BEDTIME STORIES FOR GROWNUPS

VOLUME 1

WEBSTER RUSSELL & DEE COFFEEN

All rights are reserved. In accordance with the U.S. Copyright Act of 1976, the scanning, uploading, and electronic sharing of any part of this book, without the permission of the authors constitute unlawful piracy and theft of the author's intellectual property. If you would like to use material from the book (other than for review purposes), prior written permission must be obtained by contacting the authors, at russanddeebook@icloud.com.
Thank you for your support of the authors.

C & R Publications 2020 Copyright

© Webster Russell & Dee Coffeen

The rights of Webster Russell and Dee Coffeen have been asserted

Print ISBN: 979-8-35093-216-4
eBook ISBN: 979-8-35093-217-1

Printed in the United States of America

OTHER BOOKS:

The Wizard Of Barkler's Hard

Dance Until the Music Ends

The Almost Perfect Murder

Harry and the Stock Tank Dragon

The Second Time Around:

A Guide Through the Maze of Internet Dating

A Second Time Around: A Love Story

PHOTO JOURNALS

Pictures That Inspire Stories

Antarctica: A Land of Stark Beauty

Alaska: A Land of Wonder

Egypt: The Land of Pharaohs

The Amazon

Venice

BOOKS BY WEBSTER RUSSELL

The Time Between The Numbers

Healthcare's Next Tsunami

WHY DID WE WRITE THIS BOOK

Isaac Asimov wrote in his series "Foundation", "Stories become burdens if left untold." These stories are not burdens to us however we feel the need for them to be told.

Having said that, we usually ask this question in our non fiction books. We do this to give you, the reader, a view into the our mind and the theory we are trying to articulate.

There is no theory we wish to postulate within these pages. This book is the result of a series of "Brain Farts". A brain fart is "A temporary mental lapse or failure to reason correctly." As you read some of these stories you may believe this to be true.

Now why did we write this book? Truthfully it was one of our quirky ideas that we got on a cruising sea day. We had not come across this storybook concept before. That doesn't mean that you may not be able to find some books out in the vast Kindle or Apple libraries.

The short stories you will find in this book do not fit into a specific genre. We found it more fun and challenging to write in different genres. In this book you will find fantasy, science fiction and stories taken from today.

We hope you enjoy the stories housed between these covers.

WHY SHOULD YOU READ THIS BOOK?

The answer to this question is, you should read this book because the story's are short, of different genres, they are easy to read and we would like you to buy it.

As we said, the stories fall into several genres, science fiction, a bit weird, philosophical, fantasy, or just a story with heart.

In any case, our greatest hope is that you enjoy the stories that are tucked between these covers and will tell others.

One more thing (thanks Apple). As you read this, we are writing Volume II. Our plan is to have this next volume published in December of 2024.

I AM A WORD

I Am A Word

The philosopher Alva Noë wrote, "Perception is not something that happens to us, or in us. It is something we do." With that in mind let me introduce myself, I am a word. You and I are inseparable although you won't admit it. Without me you are without thought, or communication. You are without love or anger and you can not learn or teach. This may sound egotistical but without me you are just another thing in this vast world.

Alone I am useful, strung together, I am a thought or concept. You see I am the building block of all your processes, your society and your beliefs.

I have been a part of you since the dawn of man. Your creator made me available to you, and you created me, however, in truth your use of me controls every aspect of your life.

I exist in many languages, about sixty five hundred to be precise. Humanity only sought to document me however about fifty five hundred years ago in Mesopotamia now known as Iraq. I have been found carved on rocks, painted, carved on walls and on clay tablets, written on parchment, printed in books, and now I am made up of ones and zeros on electronic tablets, phones and computers. This ability to document life and discoveries by using me, created the ability for you to pass on learning through the ages.

I define science and I define religion. I make it possible for you to create, describe, and share.

Without me you couldn't describe the beauty of a sunset or the pain of a loss. The likes of Shakespeare and Steven King have used me for self aggrandizement, wealth as well as to entertain you. Jacques Cousteau and Michio Kaku used me to theorize and teach.

Without me you would still be fighting over mates, food, and territory. Without me, there would be no peace only subjugation via fear and strength.

Without me there would be no scientific thesis, medicine, philosophy, or for that matter society`, there would just be autonomic reactions to external stimuli.

My judicious use can create new worlds in your mind. My use can share memories and lessons with your family and others. Using me can form friendships and love affairs. Just as easily the non judicious use of me can produce the opposite reactions.

I am strong yet I am also weak. My power comes from my use and your understanding of that use. My weakness comes from the same concept, so use me carefully.

Remember, you are not alone in using me, you are just one of many. Many species use me in more rudimentary ways. There are also some species that use me in more sophisticated ways then you.

I may sound self centered, but that is because of my importance to your life. Understand me and the universe can be yours. Reject me and fall back into chaos.

FORM 300

Form 300

CHAPTER 1

As you read this story, do not make assumptions about its narrative. You may insert your biases if you wish. This story, however, is written in an open context, or, in short, without color.

* * * * * *

When you hear the words "Form 300," the thought of a governmental form comes to mind. If that was your first inkling, you would be correct. It is not just any government form; it is a form that may well control the opportunities in your life.

Form 300 is the product of Franny Franklin's death. She died, mysteriously, late one night in an alley in one of our large eastern cities. A witness, yet to be identified, said it was racist in nature. Politicians at the local, state, and federal levels voiced their outrage, which echoed widely in the absence of first-hand evidence and facts. All levels of racial inequities were laid at the feet of this death; however, "social and racial injustice" seemed to gain the most traction, so much so that the cultural mode switched from equality and meritocracy to equity, from equality of opportunity to equality of outcome, with governmental help, of course.

The political uproar over this death resulted in the passing of the Franny Franklin Act. The Act required all citizens over the age of sixteen to get their DNA tested. The results of that test would be placed on Form 300, with the most prominent race noted first and other racial components descending in order. The results would be forwarded to both state and federal databases to be used as laws were developed. This law stated that the Form 300 had to be carried with you at all times.

A later law required that the form be used to assure equity in hiring, home purchases, college admissions, advancement considerations, bank loans, governmental grants, scholarships, academic grading, and, as the law put it, "any other situation where a social justice issue could arise."

One of those "radicals" was a man named Johnathon Wiley. Johnathon was not your average guy. He held a PhD in biochemistry and a second one in electrical engineering, both from MIT. Add to that, he could make a computer do anything his mind could dream of. To all that knew of his mental prowess, he was a man to be reckoned with. What made this man even more unique was that he did not suffer under the law; in fact, he was a recipient of the policy's largess.

The question then is: Why did he become the man whose goal was to radically change society's norms, and what did he do?

Johnathon was one of the blessed in the country. His Form 300 stated that his DNA showed his racial makeup to be one of the top two "victims of social injustice." Irrespective of his status within society, he worked hard; his discoveries were important, and his peers had great respect for him. After graduation, he became a research professor at one of the country's leading universities. During his years there, he became an expert in the manipulation of the human DNA using newly discovered RLR techniques. Those techniques led to the discovery of systems whose mass production and implementation could create DNA changes.

What drove him to become one of the underground was that the "non-chosen" wondered aloud if his acceptance into MIT and his subsequent degrees were because of his brilliance and hard work or a result of his Form 300 results. That thought bothered him greatly. Knowing what he had sacrificed to achieve what he had was known only to himself, and in his mind, it meant nothing to the society as a whole.

Through his work, hereditary diseases that plagued his race were going to be eradicated. Little did anyone realize that his work and success would help change the social makeup of the world he lived in.

* * * * * * * *

Quietly, over the years, he built a world-class lab in the basement of his mountain home. He operated under Washington surveillance, saying, "If they can't see you, they can't shoot you."

His "thefts" were masked by his successes. Those that watched these things just thought that he needed to replace his equipment, secondary to wear and tear. Then, of course, if someone thought about accusing him of wrongdoing, the claim of racism might be raised, squashing the complaint. These "procurements" still created a feeling of paranoia within him. After all, he had walked off with hundreds of thousands of dollars of expensive equipment and glassware, piece by piece. Then came the chemicals. They were much harder to steal because the need was great and the supply came in small containers. He couldn't take them in quantity, as it could show up as abnormally high use and raise questions.

Finally, he was ready. The equipment was installed, operating within tolerances, the chemistry was documented and successfully compiled, and his theory simulated as best he could. If his work proved successful, it would change his world forever.

CHAPTER 2

It took over a year to complete step one of his secret projects. What took time and patience was contacting someone in the resistance who could make decisions.

Because of the way the resistance was compartmentalized, he was the only one aware of the project's ultimate goal. The one component that was out of his control was the establishment of a block chain–based database. Security was an operational priority. Per protocol, Johnathon had no awareness of who was in the chain of information or command. Without over-the-top security, he would certainly be discovered; the equipment and chemicals he had stolen would result in him facing major felonies and potentially death.

While the security protocols were put into place, he quietly developed the chemical makeup of the shot that was the basis of his theory. Phase one consisted of animal tests for efficacy and safety. He was using mice as test subjects. He created both a control group and an equal group of injected mice. At the end of this phase, the efficacy rate was less than he hoped for; however, the safety factor was excellent. After running the data through a sophisticated algorithm and AI software, changes to the shot's "cocktail" were recommended. Once the "cocktail" was recomposed, he repeated the phase with new mice. Two weeks later, blood was drawn. The safety results remained excellent, and the final Phase 1 data set showed that his Crisper project had 97 percent efficacy.

He then let the males and females of the test group "get together." The idea was to see if the changes that occurred in the test group were transferred to their progeny.

Three weeks later, the first brood was born. Each young mouse had blood drawn and tests done. Irrespective of the automatic systems he designed, it took time to run the test and for the AI software to correlate the data.

The data showed that the results of the shot were transferred. It was an amazing feat, considering this work was carried out at night and on weekends.

Unlike TV programs, science is like a hospital emergency room, with moments of chaotic excitement punctuated by hours of quiet and boredom. Every success and discovery Johnathon made was followed by the slow and dull process of testing that theorem. Each theorem led to another discovery and another theorem to be tested. Each proven theorem was like a piece in a jigsaw puzzle, and over time, the puzzle took shape. The more the pieces fit together, the faster the puzzle completion was achieved.

After two years of tedious work, all but one piece of the puzzle was left to be put in place. That puzzle piece that was still absent from the puzzle was human testing.

With data in hand, he was ready for "Phase 2" of the project. Phase 2 was a small human trial to evaluate both efficacy and safety in humans. This was not an easy task, given how compartmentalized the opposition was.

The government was very intrusive and had its tendrils well into society. On the other side of the equation, the opposition was much better organized than anyone believed. They communicated via old, untraceable technology, used chronically adapted e-sims, and used the dark web exceptionally well. It doesn't mean they did everything perfectly. They were highly agile, exceptionally strategic, very compartmentalized, and always seemed to be a couple of steps ahead of the government, but every once in a while, someone got caught.

Early on, the opposition heavily recruited a number of the "unchosen," who were brilliant coders and hackers. Their job was to "listen" to the government and change things if it was in the plan so as to further the opposition's agenda.

Determined to move to Phase 2 testing, Johnathon contacted his connection to the underground to seek at least two hundred healthy men and women of childbearing age. One of the opposition's requirements was that the volunteers had to come from all the states, randomly placed within the state. Much to his surprise, it took less than two months to get the volunteers he needed. The volunteers were then divided into groups of ten, and their data was compartmentalized to keep the overall information safe. Like everything else, the supply chain for the shot's distribution and its injection was given to each volunteer in a random manner. The data he was to get would be protected by the opposition's block-chain technology.

Thank goodness for computers, which, with their software, gave insight into the chaos of this data. Although it doesn't take six months for his inoculation to do its magic, Johnathon decided to wait that long before starting the follow-up blood draws.

His human trial data proved a success; in that, it proved, at least for the short term, that his shot proved his theory and was both effective and safe. Johnathon decided to forgo a Phase 3 trial. After a secure video conference, the underground decided it was time to start full bore into "Project Change."

The implementation of "Project Change" was a three-step process. Step one: shots would be given. Step two: members of the opposition hack into the state and federal databases and insert the new data into the databases over time. The project recipients report that the data on their Form 300 may have been hacked, and they request a retest. If their data was different from the original test, it was repeated, and they would receive a new Form 300. As the word traveled through the opposition's communication network, demand grew. To cover the growing number of changes, the opposition's hackers created a findable hack into the system, placing in the public the belief that the data were not safe, much less correct.

Within eighteen months, the Form 300 effect on society was in chaos and crumbling in importance.

You see, Project Change's whole purpose was to collapse Form 300's importance to society's push for equity. The changes created by Johnathon Wiley were to, over time, bring neutrality to DNA. In short, the minority and majority became so close from a DNA standpoint that their social value was nil. Form 300 and its political creations collapsed, as did victimhood, virtue signaling, and the educational programs that promoted these issues. Much to the great disappointment of the media and many politicians, the belief in meritocracy and equality overcame the false philosophy of equity.

GRONK THE MAGNIFICENT

Gronk the Magnificent

CHAPTER 1

Jenny was a bright and precocious little girl. At three years old, she had the run of her domain and commanded all within it. The rulers, Mom and Dad, had certain rules that she was not allowed to violate: she must eat her meals; she must take a nap; and her bedtime occurred at certain times.

Jenny's great fear was that as she got older, the number of rules would increase, but that was for another day. She heard the grandfather clock in the hallway strike eight, and she knew what came next.

The words of her parents floated into her kingdom. What was frustrating was that neither doors nor walls stopped them.

"Jenny, go and brush your teeth and get ready for bed. Remember, I will check your toothbrush. Now get going." It didn't do any good to ask for five more minutes because the answer was invariably "NO. Now get going," her mom would say. She thought it odd that her dad never ordered her to bed. In spite of that, she also knew that if he ever did get after her, she was in real trouble.

Bedtime was awful. She was a busy girl with lots of important things to do. On top of that, bedtime was boring. Mom and Dad would come in, tuck her in, give her a hug and kiss, turn on the nightlight, and ceremoniously, if not joyously, shut the door and head back to the kitchen. She, on the other hand, would just lay there, staring at the ceiling. Tonight, however, was going to be different. Tonight was going to affect the rest of her life.

* * * * * * * *

Jenny was sure she had been staring at the ceiling for hours when she heard a commotion and then some grunting under her bed. She had the type of personality that didn't scare easily. In this case, she was a bit indignant. Something was under her bed without her permission, and that was not allowed. Well, Mom and Dad were different.

"Get out here or show yourself," she ordered.

That demand was followed by more grunting. This time, however, her bed moved.

"Stop that, and come out now," she ordered again.

"Listen, quit ordering me about; I am moving as fast as I can. There isn't a lot of room down here," came a low, rumbling voice.

With that, Jenny's bed lurched upward and came back down with a thump. Standing at the foot of her bed was this ugly "thing." It did, however, have sad-looking "eyes."

Sitting up in her bed with her hands on her hips, Jenny asked, "What are you doing under my bed?"

"Aren't you afraid of me?" This thing asked, then growled, and then he attempted to look as fearful as possible.

"You're kidding, right? Why would you ask that?" Jenny asked.

"Look at me; I am scary-looking, and my voice sends chills through people." The thing said.

Jenny looked at him. Well, he was big; he was an awful shade of green; he had yucky bumps all over, a huge mouth, sharp, menacing teeth, and a really bad breath, she thought. "You know, aside from your really bad breath, you are just not that scary."

A look of disappointment shrouded the monster's face. "Don't feel bad. Mom and Dad say I don't scare easily. Maybe you just need a friend. Do you want a friend?" Jenny asked.

"I've never had a friend before. I am not sure I know how to be a friend," the monster said.

Jenny crawled to the end of her bed. When she got to the end of her mattress, she stood up so she could look the monster in the face.

"If you want, I will teach you, but it's gonna be hard. Making friends takes a lot of work, so are you sure you want to do this?" Jenny asked with her hands firmly placed on her hips.

"Okay, but you can't tell your parents. They will want you to send me away," the monster said.

"That will be hard because I tell my parents everything. So, because we are going to be friends, I will keep our secret. Now I'm Jenny; what is your name?"

The monster stood as tall as he could. He took on an almost-regal pose, looked down at her, and said, "Gronk the Magnificent."

"Hi Gronk," Jenny said. "I have to go to sleep now, so get back under the bed, and I will see you tomorrow." With that, Jenny walked on her mattress to the head of her bed and slipped her feet under the covers. She fluffed up her pillows, laid down, and pulled up her covers up to her chin.

"Good night, Gronk; sweet dreams." Jenny said.

"Good night, Jenny," came a rumbling voice from under the bed. The room quieted to only the sound of breathing from a little girl and the monster that lived under her bed.

CHAPTER 2

Friendship was a difficult concept for Gronk to learn; after all, he had been a scary monster of the night for more than one hundred years. Jenny, however, was a patient teacher. In truth, they learned together.

What made it more difficult was that as Jenny grew older, her idea of friendship changed as well. The truth is, they were more than friends; they were more like a sister and brother . Gronk was a great listener, and he was very nonjudgmental. She trusted him absolutely and was constantly amazed at his wisdom and compassion.

As Jenny grew older, she made many new friends, yet every evening, they talked while she sat on the bed and Gronk on the floor. Jenny was now fifteen. Over the twelve years of their "friendship," her parents seemed oblivious. They did notice, however, how mature, focused, intelligent, and well-balanced Jenny had become. A lot of the credit, she told herself, was because of Gronk.

Then there were boys. That was a tough time for both of them. Gronk could see that "boys" seemed to take more of her time and attention. Inevitably, one evening, she came home crying. Gronk heard her tell her mom and dad that David, whoever he was, broke up with her.

After talking with her parents, she came upstairs, still crying. "What's wrong? Who's David?" Gronk asked as he came out from under the bed.

"I don't want to talk about it," Jenny said, in between sobs.

"I thought friends never kept secrets," Gronk said.

"Gronk, you wouldn't understand. I was in love with him, and he broke it off. He hurt me when he did that."

Gronk may not have understood the word or the concept of love, but he knew the word hurt. "He hurt you?" Gronk said in an angry voice. Raising up to his full height and looking like the monster he truly was, he said, "Tell me where he is at. He will pay a huge price for hurting you."

Jenny had never seen Gronk angry, and she hoped to never see it again. His anger gave him the ability to stand a good seven feet tall. His eyes glowed bright red, and his body took on a muscular tone that no bodybuilder could ever match. With each breath came a cloud of what looked like steam, and his teeth gleamed. For the first time in the twelve years she had known him, she was scared of who he was and what he could do.

Jenny knew that she had to calm down and then calm Gronk down, if for no other reason than to save David's pitiful life.

"Gronk. David didn't hurt me like he hit me or anything. He broke my heart." Well, that was the wrong thing to say because Gronk became more agitated with those words.

"Gronk, I thought I loved David, and I thought he loved me, but he didn't. Do you understand love, Gronk?" Jenny said.

With the question, she could see him calm down a bit. "No," he said.

"Love is a lot like friendship, except it is more intense. I am no real expert, but I will try to explain it to you.

There are several kinds of love. I love you like a brother. I would never do anything intentionally to hurt or disappoint you. I would never lie to you, and I love talking to and being with you.

There is the love that I have for my parents. It is similar to what I feel for you, but stronger. We have a bond that only a family can feel. It is an instinctive bond that we started the day I was born.

Then there is love, which comes when you form a relationship with someone. It usually starts when you meet them, and there is a chemistry between you. Now don't ask me what chemistry is, as I can't really explain it, but you know it when you feel it. If things go well, those feelings of attraction grow stronger. You usually want to please the other person because you don't want to lose them. I thought I loved David, and he loved me, but the truth was that he didn't. Tonight, he wanted to be intimate with me." Jenny knew Gronk's face like a book, and there was a question lurking behind his eyes. Jennie had to choose her words carefully so as to not rekindle his anger. "Intimate is to become physical, touching each other. He wanted to touch me in places I didn't want him to. When I said no, he got angry. We had an argument, and that is when he broke up with me. I was really hurt, but I knew one thing for sure: I didn't want to go out with him again. With the help of Mom and Dad, I realized that by saying no to him, I really hurt his ego. He and his buddies thought he was a real stud, and this girl in front of you, sitting on this bed, had the temerity and guts to say no to him. So, you see, I hurt him more than you ever could, at least where it counts.

There is one more type of love that is really important: true love. True love is a strong and lasting affection between two people. They are in a happy, passionate, and wonderful relationship. My mom and dad have that kind of love. Mom tells me that they love each other today as much, if not more than, when they got married."

By the time Jenny finished, Gronk had calmed down, and tearing David's limb from limb didn't matter as much.

CHAPTER 3

David hurting his friend never really left Gronk's mind. Hopefully, without Jenny's notice, he made sure no guy tried anything again. Gronk had learned how to appear only to the boyfriend if things started to get out of hand. It was amazing how an ugly face and a gaping maw would scare off the most ardent lover.

Then Sam came along. Gronk never really understood what it was, but he could see that there was chemistry between them. Gronk's saving grace was that Jenny went to college in her hometown, so he saw her many times over the next four years. After graduation, Jenny started teaching at the local high school, and Sam took over his dad's family business. One night, Gronk heard Jenny come through the front door, and she was crying differently, but she was crying. Gronk was sure Sam was different, but evidently not. Thinking about that, he started to get angry, but he held it in check until he heard Jenny's side of the story. After what seemed like hours, Jenny came through her bedroom door. Her crying had stopped, but her eyes were red. What was different from her incident with David was that she had a great big smile on her face. She held out her hand. It had a ring on it. So Gronk thought, She got a ring, so what?

"Gronk, Sam asked me to marry him, and I said yes. This is the happiest day in my life." Jenny said.

For the first time in the one hundred-plus years of his life, a tear rolled down his cheek. It didn't take a rocket scientist, whatever that was, to realize that the best friend he ever had, really the only friend he ever had, was going to leave him.

Jenny saw the tear on his face. For the first time in twenty years, she walked up and hugged him. At that moment, he discovered love. It was exhilarating, yet painful. The love he discovered was going to leave him.

After the hug, she stepped back and took his huge hand in hers, looked him in his big red eyes, and said, "We are not through yet, you, big oaf. We'll talk about what's next in a few days."

True to her word, two evenings later, Jenny sat on the floor next to the monster that had been her best friend for twenty years. "When Sam and I get married, we will be moving into his family home. I want you to come with me. You can't sleep under our bed, though." She took a big breath. "I know you can get larger, but can you get smaller?" Jenny asked.

"Yes," Gronk answered. "I can fit into one of your suitcases if I have to."

"Okay. One day, I will want you to get into a suitcase, so we can get you over to our new house." Jenny said

"Should I hibernate?" Gronk asked.

"You can hibernate?" she asked.

"Sure. How did you think I stayed quiet under your bed? I hibernated at that time for five years. Your mom and dad were pretty busy the first two years of their marriage, so your mom didn't wake me until you were three." Gronk said.

"You knew my mom? Why didn't you tell me that? All these years I kept our secret, and you never told me." Jennie said.

"Your mom made me promise not to tell you, so our friendship would be just ours. Also, when I hibernate, I lose some of my memories. When you came up and told me about Sam and your memories, my time with your mother came flooding back." Jenny just smiled. "Oh, Mom and I are going to have one serious talk.

Tell you what, let's get you in that suitcase and get you hibernating, so we can get you over to our new home."

******

As we all know, when we sleep, we have no sense of time. Because Gronk had no dreams, his memories of the past twenty years started to disappear. One sunny day, someone was shaking his body, and he became aware of a sweet, familiar, and lyrical voice calling his name. He opened his big red eyes, and there was a beautiful young woman that looked familiar. Beside her was a man.

"Gronk, it is me, Jenny, the little girl you befriended twenty-two years ago. This is my husband, Sam. I told him all about you, so he wanted to meet you."

It took Gronk a few minutes to unwind from the suitcase and stand up and stretch. He looked around. It looked like he had hibernated in their basement, not that it really mattered.

Jenny took his hand. "You have been sleeping long enough, and it is time for you to get back to work." Jenny said.

Jenny and Sam led Gronk up and out of the basement and up a flight of stairs into a bedroom. In the bedroom, against a wall, was a crib. Standing in the crib was a one-year-old little boy. Seeing Gronk, the little boy jumped up and down, and what sounded like a bellow to Gronk came from the little one.

"Gronk, this is Joseph, our son, and your new friend. You two better make friends quickly because you have only had him for eighteen to twenty years." Jenny said. Smiling, she and Sam headed down stairs while Joseph laughed, jumped up and down, and the seven-foot, red-eyed, green-colored "monster" just stood there with a big smile on his ugly face.

THE STORY TELLER

CHAPTER 1

Let me introduce myself. I am Dauid Boyle. I am a storyteller. I have lived among people in a small port community called "Ullapool" on the west coast of Scotland for sixty-five summers. For all intents and purposes, my village really became known in 1788 as a herring fishing port of some note. Prior to becoming known for our herring fishing, our village was only an insignificant hamlet made up of just over twenty households.

My mother was unusual in two ways. First, she could read and write, which was unusual in our time. Secondly, she was known as a storyteller far and wide. My father was a successful farmer. Together, we lived better than most in our village. Fortunately, or unfortunately, I was their only child. The fortunate part was that my mother insisted I learn to read and write. The unfortunate part was that I had no siblings.

I never had any desire to follow in my mother's footsteps; in fact, I loved farming. I loved the feel of earth in my hands and the beauty of the spring plantings as they poked out of the earth; however, my world was going to change. On the night of my seventh birthday, I was awakened from my sleep by a bright light and soft voices that seemed to come from a group of gray figures that surrounded my bed. I could not see any of them clearly or make out their features very well. They looked taller than most of the "people" I had ever seen. They wore grey cloaks with hoods that partially hid their faces. The skin that I could see was a lifeless grey color, and their eyes were black as the moonless night. At first, I was scared. One of the figures stepped toward me and pulled back his hood. His hair and beard were long and colorless as well. If it were not for the beard, I could not tell if it was a man or woman standing before me. It smiled at me and placed its hand on my shoulder. In a calm voice that rose above the din, it said, "Do not be afraid. Everything will be alright. We are here to help you start your journey to become a storyteller."

"I don't want to be a storyteller. I want to be a man of the land." I said

"You were chosen at birth, and now you must fulfill your fate." It said.

As its words stopped, a sudden calm came over me, and I was not able to move a muscle. The many voices blended into one and weaved their way into my mind. I don't know how much time went by because the next thing I knew was awaking with the sun shining in my small window and the sounds of birds in the air.

Was it a dream or a hallucination that I had? I was confused. I got out of bed, quickly got dressed, pushed aside the curtain that separated my space from the area where my mother cooked our meals, and walked toward her. As she turned toward me, I saw that a golden glow surrounded her. For a moment, she just stared at me.

"I see you have been visited for the first time by what I call "the visitors." Are you alright?" she asked.

"I am still a bit scared and confused. How do you know of my visit?" I asked

"The glow of a chosen storyteller now surrounds you. The visitors came to me as well last night and told me that you started your journey," my mother said.

"Why didn't you tell me about this?" I asked.

"Because you must be chosen. Until that happens, telling you would serve no purpose.

Your father knows about what happened last night, so he will not need your help today.

Now come over to the table and sit in a chair, and I will tell you what a storyteller does and what to expect. It is more than you think." My mother said, motioning to a chair at the table where they eat.

"Can everyone see the glow?" I asked.

"No, only other storytellers can see it. Now sit down and listen," my mother said.

CHAPTER 2

My mother walked over to another chair at our dinner table and sat down. She took in a deep breath and brushed her hair back. The glow that surrounded her pulsed slowly. The pulsing glow hypnotically drew my attention toward listening to her. Her voice became melodic, soothing, and mesmerizing. The world's sounds slowly disappeared, leaving only her voice in my ears.

"Let me start by saying that you will be entering another world. More importantly, your life is no longer your own; it now belongs to others. There is no way I or your father can prepare you for what your future will bring. The life of each storyteller is different. The challenges you will face will be different from those who came before you. The expectations laid before you will be like wisps of smoke. You will see them, but the clarity will not be there. All is not lost, however. The stories you will learn and the visions you will be offered will pave the road way to your future.

There are some things that are common to our experiences. You will never suffer from hunger or thirst. You may well receive the power of the calming voice that you hear now. The stories and the attributes you will acquire will always be rewarded. You will be seen as someone of special status. You will be praised; however, you must remain humble. Humility can only be learned and constantly practiced. As you grow older, find yourself a wife who can hold your feet to the ground.

Last night, you received your first set of stories. These are stories of our people and history. Although some of us can read and write, we pass down our histories through stories. In fact, these stories define who and what we are.

As you grow older, you will discover that storytelling is a dramatic art. Like any art, you will learn from your failures. Over time, you will learn how to make those listening to you hear, see, and smell the stories you tell. Remember this: history and the stories you tell are a narrative stringing one person to another, one event to another, and one time to another. Because of that, when you tell our stories, differentiate history from myth.

Do you know what myth is?" my mother asked.

"I think so." I said.

"A myth is a story that usually has no known origin. The listener makes no attempt to justify a mystical story, even though it does not seem plausible. The people who hear it just trust what they have heard the storyteller say is true.

A truth is something you learn through challenge. Each storyteller embellishes the story a little, so, in truth, it becomes more of a myth over the passage of time. What must not change is that the stories must always reflect our beliefs and culture. Always stay true to them," my mother said.

"So you are prepared; what happened last night will happen many times over your lifetime. I must also tell you that the visitors told me that you have been chosen to be one of the very few who see the future. This is a tremendous responsibility that is being placed on you. If what you see makes you believe we must change the course of our lives, it cannot be told through edict, but by the use of parables and mentoring," she said.

"Mother, what good is it to see "the future" if I cannot tell others exactly what I have seen?" I asked.

My mother smiled and said, "You may well interpret what you see improperly. When that happens, and it will, you will be seen as one who only seeks power. Son, you are not listening. I said you cannot tell anyone specifically what you see or hear. You may, however, use your other talents to create the things you wish to achieve."

"What other talents?" I asked.

"Seek answers for this and other questions from the visitors. They will help you only if you ask for it," mother said.

✴ ✴ ✴ ✴ ✴ ✴

This conversation with my mother was held so many years ago, yet, to me, it was just yesterday.

I can truthfully say much has happened since that day. I should also tell you that I have never been more than two sunrises away from where I sit right now, yet I know thousands of stories that come from all over the known world because of the visitors. That, however, is for another time.

As I have intimated, my story does not end with these words. The wondrous things I have learned, the challenges I have faced, and the things I have seen would fill a book, and that is the quandary I face. My life has revolved around the power of the spoken word. That being true, over the years, I have also learned the lasting impact of the written word. I have yet to master it, so my writing progress is slow.

My years on this earth are many, so I tire easily, and I must rest. Hopefully, we will get together at another place and time, and then I will tell you my greatest story, the story of my life. It will be worth the wait.

Be well.

A MAN NAMED CHARLIE

This Is The Story Of A Man Named Charlie

CHAPTER 1

This is the story of a man named Charlie Sledge—an usual name for an unusual man. Charlie was a man in his sixties, slightly built, with grey in his hair. Almost every day, rain or shine, you can find him sitting in the middle of an old wood bench, on the edge of a fairly large lake, which sits in the middle of a city park, in the middle of a small American city.

Charlie, at best, looks sad, and, at worst, he looks emotionally crushed. He sits quietly and unmoving on that wooden bench, staring out at the ducks and geese as they float by.

One day, a young man walked slowly by the bench. What seemed unusual was that the young man was dressed in a light shirt and slacks, even though it was the middle of November.

Seeing Charlie in apparent distress, the young man turned around and walked over to where Charlie was sitting. Looking empathetically at him, he quietly asked, "Excuse me, sir, are you alright?"

Charlie looked back at him and said, "No, I am not. I've had a big loss in my life. What's worse is that I may be partially responsible for that loss, and that fact weighs heavily on my soul. The good news is, if you can call it that, I learned one of life's major lessons."

"Is there anything I can do for you?" the young man asked.

Charlie just patted the bench beside him, inviting the young man to sit down. "I'm going to tell you a story. I hope that this story will help you learn the lesson I had to learn the hard way." The young man walked over to the bench and sat down.

Charlie took in a deep breath and then said, "Many years ago, I met the love of my life. It was a quick romance. We ended up at the Justice of the Peace's office two weeks after we met. Jen, that was my wife's name, and I had a long, wonderful, and loving marriage. We had one son we named Scott. Scott was a wonderful boy who was everything we had hoped for. He has now grown into a wonderful man, husband, and father.

Eighteen years ago, doctors diagnosed Jen with a terminal disease. In spite of all their efforts and expertise, the sickness quickly overtook her. One afternoon, as I lay beside her on our bed, holding her hand, she opened her eyes, looked up at me, smiled, took my other hand in hers, and said, 'Charlie, it's time. I have to go.'

"I begged her to stay, but she said, 'No, it's just time,' and she asked me to kiss her. Just after we kissed, she took in a breath, let it out, her hand let go of mine, and she died."

The young man noticed the profound look of sadness cross Charlie's face. Charlie took in a breath, and then he continued, "I was lost; I didn't know what to do without her. The funeral came and went. The truth is, I really don't remember much about it.

I just sat in my recliner, staring at the wall. Nothing seemed to interest me anymore. One afternoon, my son, his wife, and grandson came over to the house to see if I was okay. You know, kids are really intuitive. Little Scotty saw that "Grandpa" was sad. He ran over to me on his little two-year-old feet. He grabbed my leg and said, 'Grandpa, I know you miss Grandma. You know that I love you, Daddy loves you, and Mommy loves you, but I love you the most.'" Tears came to Charlie's eyes.

"That little boy's words and smile shone a small light into my heart, and a bit of the pain I felt eased as well."

"I love you, Grandpa," little Scotty said again. "Are you going to be okay? At that moment, I knew that things were going to be better."

Charlie's face eased a bit. "The next morning, the birds chirped a teensy bit louder, and the sun seemed a little brighter. I got up, showered, got dressed, made my coffee, and started the short walk to my son's house. Just as I turned onto their walkway, Scotty burst out the front door, yelling, 'Grandpa, Grandpa,' then he hugged my leg and said, 'Hi, Grandpa. What are we going to do today?' I hadn't thought about that. It became clear that Scotty expected me to have a plan for the day. Every night, I sat at the kitchen table and planned our next day's activities. What was wonderful was that each time I planned the next day's activities, a bit of the grim shroud was lifted off my heart. What was even more amazing was that, at least in my mind, I discussed the next day's plans with Jen, which made my day even happier."

As Charlie was talking, a smile crossed his face. "Before I knew it, little Scottie wasn't little anymore, and because of school, our visits went from all day to mornings, afternoons, and weekends. I still made sure I got to his house in time to see him get on the school bus and head off to school."

"Those were wonderful days. I found a new joy in going to the park to watch the mothers and children run and play while, at the same time, feeding the ducks and geese. About 2:30 p.m., my internal alarm clock went off, and I would head back to my son's house to meet Scotty as the school bus let him off.

Time just flew by, and the next thing I realized, Scotty had turned sixteen, and he had his own car. Sixteen or not, I still saw him off to high school each morning. Scotty's car not only met his needs and wants, but it helped me as well. I was finding it tough to get to the grocery store as well as get some chores done. Faithfully, Scotty was there to help me clean up the yard, mow the lawn, and take me grocery shopping. Life was great."

The young man noticed a look of despair come over Charlie's face as he continued to speak. "One morning, at about 2:00 a.m., I was awakened by a hand being placed on my shoulder. Much to my surprise, I felt no fear or anxiety. I turned my head to the left, where the hand came from, and

I saw a ghost-like figure standing by my bed. 'Charlie,' it said in a quiet, soothing voice, 'It's your time.'

Those three words sent a shock through me. I knew I would hear them at some point, but now was not the time."

As much as Charlie tried to hide it, the young man saw a flash of fear in Charlie's eyes. "Listen, I can't leave yet; I have too much to do." Charlie stopped for a moment. The soothing voice repeated his message. "Charlie, it's your time."

"There has got to be a way to delay my time. I want to be with my family a bit longer." Charlie said.

"Are you sure you want to put this off? I cannot leave empty-handed," the voice said.

"There must be someone who is sick you can take," Charlie implored.

"Let me ask you again. Are you sure you want to delay your time?" the voice asked.

"Yes," Charlie said emphatically.

"Until your time comes again," the apparition said, then it disappeared.

Charlie went right back to sleep, if he was even awake. The next morning, he awoke at 6:30 a.m. as usual. He showered and fixed his breakfast and coffee. He then headed out the door to see Scotty off to school. As he turned the corner to head to his son's house, he saw several cars around his son's house. Charlie assumed it was Scotty's friends. As he turned to walk up to the house, Scotty was nowhere to be seen. A moment later, his son stepped through the door. His face was drawn, and you could see tears rolling down his face.

"Dad, Scotty died last night." His son said.

Time stopped, and the ghost-like being appeared again.

"Charlie, Scotty was ill. When you decided not to go and asked me to take someone who was sick, I chose Scotty. I told you I could not leave empty-handed, and I didn't," the apparition said.

"Just as suddenly, time restarted, and the grief hit me like a piano falling from the tenth floor. I almost collapsed under the weight of my sorrow.

"My son steadied me. 'Dad, Scotty was sick, and he didn't want you to know. We and the doctor's were very optimistic he would overcome it, but it just wasn't meant to be,' my son said."

The young man saw that there was a definite sadness in Charlie's voice. "It has been a year since Scotty's death. His death, and my part in it, has all but destroyed me. I live in my recliner or come here and sit on the bench, waiting for my time to come. It never comes. My word to you is, if your time comes, don't try to delay it because of the unintended consequences."

The young man put a hand on Charlie's shoulder.

"Charlie, your life isn't over, and your time is not coming any time soon." As the young man spoke, Charlie realized the soft voice he heard seemed very familiar to him.

"Your son and his wife are going to have a baby girl. That little girl doesn't know how much she needs her grandfather; Scotty knew. Now you can see why I never came for you."

With those words, the young man slowly diffused into nothing. After a moment, the words he had just heard sunk in, and a smile crossed his face.

Today, you can find Charlie sitting in the middle of an old wooden bench, on the edge of a fairly large lake, which sits in the middle of a city park, which is located in the middle of a small American city.

Instead of a sad face, you will see Charlie wearing a big smile as he watches a little girl running around the bench he is sitting on. As she runs past him, she gives him a big, loving grin, while at the same time she is throwing small chunks of bread to the ducks and geese that are floating by.

PEG LEG BILL

CHAPTER 1

In the 1860s, it was not unusual to find a single mother whose home was on the outskirts of a community. Keep in mind that what is now the outskirts was once a house far from town. In this case, the house was home to a widow, Sarah, and her twelve-year-old son, Johnathan.

East of their cabin was the Atlantic Ocean; south and southwest of the cabin was a large expanse of forest; and to the west was the town. The widow's husband had carefully placed their home just behind the apex of the hill and close to the forest to protect it from the winter and summer storms that were known to occasionally and surprisingly rip through this part of the world.

Just after Johnathan tenth birthday, his father died. He was injured while cutting wood for winter, got an infection, and died two weeks later. Sarah and Stephen, with little help from the town, buried their husband and father on the hill to the east of their cabin.

It was now up to a ten-year-old boy and a thirty-year-old woman to do what was necessary to survive. The town was not terribly friendly. The civil war had just ended, leaving differences in place, which created difficult times within communities.

They were pretty well prepared for the first winter. With the arrival of spring, Sarah had to master plowing and planting. Although Stephen had been handling guns since he was seven, his skills as a hunter were limited. More often than not, he returned empty-handed. Daily, he and his mom were forced to decide whether to hunt or help work the fields.

Because the spring and summer's weather was unusually good, their work in the garden plot was fruitful and would help them last through the winter. What they missed was meat. They could use the chickens, but that would help in the short term but not in the long term. Stephen had to become more successful.

One day in early November, before sunrise, at the start of the rut, he headed into the forest in the hopes of getting at least one buck. Deer were plentiful this time of year, and because the bucks were calling for mates, his ability to find them was a bit easier.

He found a place with a small clearing that had a fair amount of deer scat, which, to his mind, meant the deer were nearby or, at least, had passed through.

At about sunrise, he heard some movement in the area to his right. He slowly raised his rifle and pointed it toward the sound. It wasn't long before a big buck pushed his head out of the bushes, but he stopped there. Stephen wanted a better shot, so he held off. The buck started to move away when a gun fired, and the buck dropped like a rock. Out of the tree line to his left came a deep gruff, "You waited too long, and we damn near lost the buck. It is easily seen; you have little or no idea what you are doing."

A moment later, the voice's body stepped into the clearing. He wasn't a tall man, but he was very muscular. He had a fairly long and unkept reddish-brown beard. His face was well weathered, and his clothes were worn and looked more like a sailor's than a farmer's or hunter's. He carried a sword and dagger tucked under a large, stained sash that circled his waste. The gun he carried was a really old musket. What really set him apart and was very evident was that he had a peg where his left leg should have been.

"Boy, you have got a lot to learn if you are going to hunt out here. So, what's your name, boy?" The man asked.

Johnathan just stood there, staring at this man in front of him.

"Don't be rude, boy. I asked you a question," the man said.

"Johnathan, my name is Johnathan." He said.

"Well Johnathan my name is Peg Leg Bill. Nice to meet you. Now let's gut the deer, get it home and hang the deer before the meat spoils."

"Excuse me, sir, but this is your deer. Why would you want to take it to my home?" Johnathan asked.

"Call me, Bill, son. It's obvious that there is a lot more meat here than I can eat, and I don't want it to go to waste. Not only do you look pretty scrawny, but it also looks like you might need some meat. Lastly, I bet your mother is a good cook, and truth be told, I am a terrible cook. By the way, why isn't your father out hunting instead of you?" Bill asked.

"My father died a year ago, and my mom and I share the tasks just to survive," Johnathon said.

"Another good reason for me to share this kill. Okay, let's gut it," Bill said.

Bill, like a surgeon, expertly gutted the deer, saving the liver, kidneys, and heart. Johnathon had never seen that before. The few deer he had shot, more by luck than skill, he just gutted and left the entrails in the forest. Seeing this confusion, Bill said, "The heart, liver, and kidneys can be fried up for a few good meals. We want the carcass to hang and age a bit in the cold night air. Believe it or not, it tastes better.

After they finished dressing out the deer, they found a sturdy fallen branch, tied the deer to it, and headed to the house. As they walked out of the forest, they saw Sarah in the "garden," gathering the harvest. She had planted a large one this year, both as a crop and for seeds. They didn't have the money to buy seeds in town.

Johnathon yelled at his mom as they exited the forest. "Mom, this is Bill, and look, we got a big buck."

To Sarah, the buck looked huge. Bill tipped his head toward Sarah. "With your permission, I will help your son put the deer up. First, let me properly introduce myself."

A few minutes later, they came out of the barn and headed toward the house. Sarah stood on the porch with a "mother" look on her face.

I don't want to intrude. "My name is Peg Leg Bill. Just call me Bill. I was walking through the forest when I came across this buck. I saw your son here already had a bead on it, but he was too hesitant, and I knew he would lose the shot, so I took it down. Seeing he had the bead on the deer, and I had taken it down, it would only be fair to share it, and here we are."

"Well, I appreciate what you did, Mr. . . .," Sarah said.

"Just Bill, miss," Bill said.

"Alright, Bill. We are poor, so we have nothing to pay you for your part of the deer, and we don't accept charity," Sarah said it in as proud a voice as she could muster.

"Yes, miss. I understand. I would love a cup of coffee, and then I have an idea that would help all of us," Bill said.

Sarah walked into the house, got a cup of coffee, brought it out to the porch, and handed it to Bill.

"Might I take a seat over there?" pointing to one of the rocking chairs on the porch. "My bum and leg are starting to hurt." Bill said.

Sarah pointed to the chair, and Bill climbed up on the porch, walked over to the chair, and sat down. Sarah stood there, then walked up on the porch and sat in the other chair. Johnathon sat on the stairs and watched the two of them.

"Now, there is a lot of work to get done, so let's make this quick," Sarah said, authoritatively.

"Thanks for the coffee. I have been wandering in those woods for a while, staying away from people. The truth is, I don't really like many people. When I saw your scrawny son, sorry, Johnathon, he looked like he needed some help, and I thought I might help him. He told me of your situation, and I was convinced that I might be able to help you both. Here is what I offer: I will teach your son to hunt. I will teach him how to cure the hides for use. I will teach him the ways of the forest. These skills will not only help your situation but will also free up his time to help you with the crop.

For this, I ask for a place to sleep in the barn and meals, nothing more. The benefit to me will be to have company. As soon as your son has learned what I have to teach him and you as a family are back on your feet, I will be ready to return to the forest.

All I ask is that you tell no one of my presence here. I have done nothing to place you in danger; it is just that I prefer to pick the people I engage with," Bill said.

Sarah looked sternly at Bill. "We will give it a try for two weeks and make a decision then about continuing this deal."

"Thank you, miss. I'm sorry, I forgot to give you these for dinner," Bill said. He untied a bag attached to his sash and handed it to her.

"This is the deer's heart, kidneys, and liver. The liver will make a good dinner, and the heart and kidneys will make a great soup," Bill said.

CHAPTER 2

Two weeks became two months, which grew into two years, then five years. Bill still slept in the barn, Sarah still cooked for him, and Johnathon became a very skilled hunter and woodman. As Johnathon was ready to turn seventeen, Bill said it was time for him to leave.

In the six years he had been with Sarah and Johnathon, a great deal had happened. As Johnathon's skills improved, they had more meat than they could ever use, so he took it into town and sold it. At the end of the day, he distributed what was left over to those in need. The money he earned was turned back into the farm, another horse, a better plow, seed, and a cow. The once-small garden grew. The extra produce went into town as well. Bill helped improve the cabin so it was more of a house. By the time Bill announced his leaving, Sarah and Johnathon were not rich per se, but certainly financially stable and successful. Given the family's kindness, their acceptance in town was a given. At their insistence, the townspeople did not visit often, and if they did, it was by invitation. It was only by this means that Bill's place in their lives was kept secret.

One day, Bill just disappeared. Sarah got up early as usual, made coffee, and, as she had done for the last six years, took a cup of coffee to the barn. At the barn door, she stopped and called his name. This time, however, there was no answer. Using a slightly louder voice, she said, "Bill, I have your coffee." Nothing but the sound of the chickens and a horse's whinny came back to her. Fearing something was wrong, she opened the barn door and stepped in. The place where Bill had been sleeping for the past six years was empty, and the blanket was neatly folded on one of the stalls.

Sarah ran back to the house, up the stairs, and into the front room. Johnathon was sitting at the table with a cup of coffee in his hand.

"Johnathon, Bill's gone." Sarah said. As Johnathon looked at his mother, he could see tears running down her cheeks.

Johnathon stood up and gave his mother a hug. "Mom, he said it was time for him to move on. I really wasn't ready for him to leave either. Not telling us was his way as well. I don't think he likes goodbyes. You and I will both miss him, but he helped us get in a good place and, for that, we should be thankful."

CHAPTER 3

A year had passed since Bill had left. Sarah and Johnathon thought of him often. Since he had gone, the secrecy was no longer necessary. They hired a young hand to help around the place, as the work was just too much for the two of them.

One afternoon, Johnathon was in town, getting a few things from the store his mother wanted as well as picking up a bolt of cloth that she had ordered. He had put the things in the cart that she asked for and went back into the store to settle the bill and pick up the bolt of cloth. As he settled up, the owner turned and said, "Jenny, would you please bring Miss Sarah's bolt of cloth she ordered?"

Out of the back of the store came what Johnathon considered the most beautiful girl he had ever seen.

"Is this the one, Daddy?" she asked while, at the same time, all but staring at Johnathon.

"You two have never been introduced. Johnathon, this is my daughter, Jenny. She is learning to be a teacher at the town school. Jenny, this is Johnathon. He and his mother have a very successful farm out of town. Oh, how did that bull work out for you? Did you get a calf this spring?" the store owner asked.

"Daddy, please! Johnathon, nice to meet you. Let me wrap this bolt in paper so it won't get dusty on the way out to your farm. I will bring it out to the rig when I'm finished," Jenny said, with a smile on her face.

Johnathon settled his bill, thanked the store owner, went outside, and climbed on to the buckboard's seat. It wasn't long before Jenny showed up with a neatly wrapped bolt of cloth.

"I don't mean to be forward, Johnathon, but when you come into town again, why not look me up? I will either be at the school or helping dad at the store," Jenny said.

Blushing a bit, Johnathon managed to get out, "I will." Not to show his embarrassment, he dropped the reins on the horse, and off he went back to the farm.

It took the usual fifteen minutes to get to the house, but it seemed forever to Johnathon. When he got home, he jumped down from the buckboard and ran into the house.

"Slow down. What's going on?" Sarah said.

"I met the prettiest girl in town today, and she wants to see me again," Johnathon said.

With a huge smile on her face, Sarah looked down at what she had been doing and said, "That's nice. Now bring the things in, stow the buckboard, and put up the horse and brush it down. Then tell me all about it."

It was during his third time in town that Jenny invited him to go with her to the library. She had to pick up some books for Monday's classes. The library wasn't really large, but the bookshelves were packed.

"It is going to take me a few minutes to get what I need. Why don't you look around? I just realized I never saw you in school. Do you read and write?" Jenny asked.

"Yes, Mom taught me," Johnathon said.

"Good well look around, and I will be ready to leave in a few minutes," Jenny said as she walked down the isle, created by the bookshelves.

Johnathon looked around and saw a painting in the back of the room. His curiosity got the best of him, so he walked back to look at it and see who it was. He looked up and could not believe what he saw.

"Johnathon, you ready to go?" Jenny asked

"Who is that man? I think I know him," Johnathon said.

"Really. This gentleman was a feared pirate called Peg Leg Bill, who raided this coast for years. There was a fight between him, his men and the communities around here. That battle occurred in the woods near your house. He disappeared after that battle. It was rumored he was killed; however, no one ever found his body or grave. The myth is that his ghost roams the woods, but no one has ever seen the ghost if it does exist.

I doubt then you would have ever known him, especially seeing that the fight and his reported death were over one hundred years ago."

Johnathon just stood there. *How to I explain the last six years?* he thought.

WHEN IS A DREAM A DREAM

CHAPTER 1

Samuel Goldfarb is really not a man of consequence. The truth is, he is barely known outside his apartmment building. This doesn't mean he is an introvert; he is just dull. He is a man of consistent practice. He gets up every morning at 6:30 a.m., puts on his shorts, oversized T-shirt, and running shoes, and goes for a run. Two miles later, he takes a shower, eats the same breakfast, packs the same lunch every day, and goes to work. At the end of the day, he comes home, eats the same dinner, watches a bit of TV, and goes to bed. It is when he falls asleep that he enters another life—a life that would make Walter Mitty jealous—a life that is embedded in a dream, or is it?

Before we go any further with this story, we probably should ask the question, What is a dream? To neuroscientists, dreaming is still a bit of a mystery wrapped in an enigma. Scientists say dreaming may be ". . .the interpreting of random signals from the brain and body during sleep. Some others think it is the act of consolidating and processing information gathered during the day."

In Samuel's situation, he was having what are called 'lucid dreams.' In case you don't know, lucid dreaming is when the dreamer is aware that they are dreaming. They may even have some control over their dreams. What made his dreams unusual was that each night, his dream was like a chapter in a book; it was integrated into the previous night's dream.

Unlike Walter Mitty, his "dream life" was full of questions and loneliness, except for the dog, of course.

I am getting ahead of myself, so let's start at the beginning. Samuel doesn't really remember when this "alternate reality," as he calls it, started; it just started. The dream wasn't gray or dank. What it was, was empty. There were buildings, trees, lawns, cars, and a store—just no people. It wasn't a post-war environment—just an ecosystem without humans. Food was not a problem, that is, if you didn't mind canned food. Transportation wasn't a problem, as there were cars, trucks, or buses everywhere. It was as if one weekday morning, all the people just disappeared.

The first night of this journey started with him becoming aware that he was alone. He woke up in a hotel room. That in itself was unusual, as he seldom, if ever, traveled. In this dream, it was morning. It appeared the only clothes he had were hung over a chair. There was nothing in the closet and no suitcase. On top of that, he had no idea what city or town he was in. He thought that he wasn't really old enough to suffer from dementia.

He got dressed and headed down the stairs to the hotel's lobby. Out of habit, he pushed the elevator's down button, and, to his surprise, the elevator door opened. He suddenly realized he had no idea what floor he was on. He looked above the door and saw the number four lit. Finding his room would be no problem as he propped his room's door open as he was without a key. The open door wasn't a security problem as no one seemed to be around, and there was nothing to steal anyway. Oh, well. He pushed the button for the lobby. The doors closed, and down the elevator went.

When the elevator door opened, he was struck by the fact that the lobby was completely empty. The lights were on, and the ceiling fans were turning. This was weird, and he was getting a bit uneasy. I could say frightened, but his curiosity usually overcame his fear. If people were anywhere at this time of day, it would be where they served breakfast. He looked at the signage and headed to the restaurant. He hoped the breakfast was part of the cost of his room because he had no wallet or money. When he got to the restaurant, it too was empty. The breakfast was buffet-style. To his surprise, the food was still warm, the bakery goods still soft, the coffee hot, and the juices cold. He checked the adjacent rooms to find no one. Maybe they had evacuated the hotel for some reason, and, amazingly, he slept through it. The flat-screen TV on the wall was on, but it displayed nothing but an empty studio.

Things were really getting weird, but the weirdness could wait; he was hungry, and there was food in front of him. He grabbed a plate and filled it up. He put the plate of food on the table, picked up a knife, fork, and cup, and headed for the coffee. One can't start the day without a cup of coffee. Why not splurge? He was alone, so this morning he grabbed a glass of orange juice and an extra pastry. As he looked around, he thought he saw what looked like a newspaper laying on a chair shoved under an adjacent table.

He pushed back his chair, got up, walked over to the table where he saw the paper, and picked it up. It was the Miami Herald. The date on paper was February 29, 2022, so now he had an idea where he was and when it was. He went back to "his" table and started reading the paper while he ate.

As he read, he gave up his theory of the hotel being evacuated. No firemen, policemen, or security had come back in. Aside from the sound made by his fork hitting his plate and the air conditioning, it was spookily quiet.

The paper gave no idea of anything that might cause the disappearance. There were no reports of flying saucers, great plagues, or international happenings. All he could deduce was that the "great disappearance" happened between 4:00 a.m. and 6:00 a.m. He thought that was the case because if that was today's paper, that time frame was when the paper hit the streets.

His breakfast finished, he grabbed his napkin, wiped his mouth, got up from the table, and headed back to the lobby. It was time to see if there was life beyond the hotel doors.

CHAPTER 2

Samuel decided that the hotel would serve as his "command center." The electricity was still on, and the refrigerators were still operational, so food wasn't a problem, at least for the short run.

Leaving the "breakfast room," he went downstairs into the lobby. Samuel approached the hotel's main entrance with trepidation. He looked through the glass door. Unexpectedly, he saw nothing moving. Not one person walked by, nor did a car drive by. Usually, there were taxis everywhere; today, there was nothing.

He stepped through the revolving door into a strangely quiet street. Again, his curiosity overcame any fear he might have had.

He knew a car was the best way to explore the city and countryside, so he set out to find a car with keys. Instead of a fancy Mercedes Benz, the first car he came across was a minivan with a diaper bag in the backseat, sitting next to an infant's car seat. He saw a woman's purse in the front passenger seat. He opened the driver's side door, moved the driver's seat back, and climbed in. He reached over, picked up the purse, and started a search for the keys. Her wallet had charge cards, an ID, and about $35 in cash. Pushing the lipstick and dark glasses aside, he finally found her keys and cell phone. Knowing it wouldn't matter, he dialed a number or two, but got no answer. The GPS still worked, so he dropped a pin on the hotel's position so he could find his way back later that day.

He inserted the key into the ignition and started the car. Once the gas gauge settled down, it pointed to full, probably a "Mom" thing.

He pulled the car out of its parking place and started the exploration process as it was. After a couple of hours of driving and walking, he still had not seen a single person. He did, however, find a mutt walking aimlessly around. He decided that any company was better than none, so he brought the dog into the car and set the GPS to guide him back to the hotel.

He took a different route back so he could explore further. The houses were different, the streets were different, and the landscaping was different. What did not change, irrespective of the street, was the emptiness. Not a person anywhere, yet the rudiments of an active society were everywhere.

Samuel pulled "his" car up to the hotel's front entrance and parked. It was a no-parking zone, but what the hell! There weren't any police around anywhere. Even if they were to suddenly appear, it wasn't his car anyway.

He opened the car's door, got out, and the dog jumped out and followed close behind him. Samual went up the stairs and into the lobby with the dog close on his heels. From there, it was off to the restaurant's kitchen, as neither he nor the dog had lunch.

Samuel was not a chef by any stretch of the imagination, but he could put together a meal if he had to, and he had to. The large walk-in fridge was full, as was the walk-in freezer. He grabbed some meat and veggies. The stoves were gas. He turned the "front left knob," and it lit a burner off. He found a frying pan, then found some oil and garlic powder, as well as salt and pepper. He salted the meat and threw it in the pan along with the veggies. He noticed the hotel's wine cooler on the way into the kitchen. Wine with dinner? Why not.

The dog was sitting at his feet, looking hungrily as he flipped the meat. He reached to his left, grabbed a plate and a bowl, pulled the food out of the pan, and put it on the plate. He turned, walked past the wine cooler, grabbed a bottle of red wine, and headed out to the dining room via a set of swinging doors.

He walked up to a table and sat down. He separated the plates, put a portion of the veggies and a portion of the fried meat on the second plate, and then filled the bowl with water. He picked up the second plate and the bowl and put them on the floor next to his chair. It didn't take any time for the dog to get to the plate and bowl, and it took about thirty seconds to have them clean. As Samuel watched the dog, he couldn't help but think, If that dog only understood, that filet mignon is a fine piece of meat meant to be savored, not gulped down. Oh, well, he was going to savor his.

After finishing his dinner, Samuel and "dog" headed up to his room. It had been a long day, and he was tired. He pushed open the door to his room, and the dog headed for the bed like a shot.

Samuel closed the door, walked to the bathroom, took off his clothes, hung them on the back of the bathroom door, turned on the shower, and when the water warmed up, he got in and washed up. He was never one to take long showers, so in less than five minutes, he was toweling off and heading toward the bed. The mutt had settled in on the second bed and appeared to be asleep. He walked over to his bed, sat down, and pondered what the day had been. Within a few minutes, he switched off the light, swung into bed, pulled up the covers, and fell asleep.

CHAPTER 3

It didn't seem very long before Samuel awoke. Opening his eyes came slowly, but when they were open, he quickly realized he wasn't in a hotel room, and there was no second bed or a dog. It took him a few seconds to realize that he was back in the bedroom of his house. Holy crap. I thought I knew what a lucid dream was, but that one seemed all too real, he thought.

Without thinking any more about his dream, he pulled on his running clothes and shoes and headed for the door. As usual, when he finished his run, it was into the shower, then he ate his breakfast, packed his lunch, got into his car, and headed for work.

As he drove to work, the roads were crowded, and people were everywhere. He parked his car in a garage and walked through crowded sidewalks to the building where he worked. He walked into a congested lobby and went to the elevator. He got off the elevator and walked into the office. The colleagues he worked with were at their desks. As he walked by them, they waved or spoke to him.

He worked in the IT section of the office, so his day was spent as usual, fixing personal and corporate computer issues.

After work, he headed back to his car. Unlike in his dream, he noticed the bars and restaurants were crammed with noisy, laughing people. Once he got to where his car was parked, he unlocked it, climbed in, started it, and drove home. Like in the morning when he drove into work, the roads were full of cars.

When he got home, he grabbed a beer, got his dinner ready, sat in his recliner, and, for the first time in a long time, turned on the local news. He wasn't sure what he would hear; however, his "dream" was so vivid and its surroundings so empty that he was just trying to verify life did exist here.

After dinner, he did something unusual for him: he walked the neighborhood. With joy, he saw people in their yards, sitting on their front porches, and walking their dogs. As he walked, he understood how empty his "dream" world was. Just about that time, he remembered that dreams seldom, if ever, repeated themselves. That being the case, a sense of calm came over him as he walked back to the house.

Once back in the house, he cleaned the kitchen, sat in his recliner, and turned on the TV. At about 10:30 p.m., he headed off to bed.

* * * * * * *

It seemed that as soon as he closed his eyes, he woke up again. A dog was jostling him and whining. Where in the hell did the dog come from? Then he remembered that he found the dog yesterday while having his "lucid" dream. Shit, another "day" of loneliness in another world.

He started to wonder about this dream. He went to bed last night in his house and "woke up" this morning in a hotel some three thousand miles east of his house. This was the most realistic dream he had ever experienced. The truth be known, he didn't remember ever having lucid dreams.

The dog needed to go out and do his business, and they both needed to eat, so he dressed in the same clothes he wore "yesterday" and headed for the lobby with the dog. He figured he ought to name him, so the dog became Stranger.

Stranger went outside, then came right back. They headed for the kitchen and made some breakfast. After eating and feeding Stranger, he decided it was time for some more exploring.

The electricity was still on, so gas pumps were operating. In an attempt to get gas, he used the credit card in the purse he found in the car's passenger seat. To his surprise, the card was accepted, so he filled the car's tank. After filling the tank, he went into the attached store. As everywhere else, their store was empty. He picked up two sandwiches out of the cooler along with some water and headed back to the car.

"Today," Samuel and Stranger headed further out of town. Like the day before, no people. The boredom was broken when he saw an occasional animal.

At the end of the day, rather than go back to the hotel, Samuel decided to find an empty house in a town and stay there. Food was plentiful in a local grocery store, so that wasn't an issue. With a house found, he set things up for the night. The refrigerator was operating, so he checked it and the freezer for food. There was enough in there for dinner, so he fixed dinner for both he and Stranger. He wasn't sure what to expect when his head hit the pillow. He was too tired to stay up any longer, so he turned off the light. Stranger curled up at the end of the bed. Samuel closed his eyes and drifted off.

CHAPTER 4

A moment later, he opened his eyes again to bright sunlight and the noise of a busy community. He was back on the west coast of California in his "west coast home." As he expected, there was no dog. This time, the change was not as confusing. There was a change in his attitude, however. As much as he liked the solitude of his "other" life, he missed people. Samuel had always been a loner, so this loneliness was something new in his life.

This movement between two worlds went on for a number of weeks. It was like a never-ending loop. One moment, he was in an empty Miami, and the next minute, he was in Silicon Valley with a job, a bustling community, and new friends. Even with the perception of little or no sleep, no matter which world he woke up in, he felt well rested.

There were no replays. Both stories were continuations. Each scenario was triggered by going to sleep.

As time went on, he realized his grip on reality was slipping. Sitting at his kitchen table in his Mountain View, California, home, he realized he did not know where his reality was. Was Miami, with its lack of humans and a dog, the reality, and Mountain View the dream, or was Mountain View, with its vibrance, the reality, and Miami the dream? As much as he tried, he was unable to establish what was real and what was a dream. He went so far as to entertain the thought that he was suffering from schizophrenia.

Rather than lose his mind trying to ascertain one from the other, Samuel decided to accept that both were real in their own right. Each had its joys and frustrations. One life was governed by work and societal restrictions. The other was ungoverned and driven by adventure. One life was solitude in a crowded area, and the other was friendship in a quiet, empty environment with his friend, the dog. It was truly Walter Middy-like. If he was destined to live in both worlds, he would just accept it and start to build a life in both realities.

Samuel never told anyone about this dual life. As fate would have it, Samuel was diagnosed with a terminal disease in his Mountain View reality. Even in hospice, his sleep brought his Miami life back to him. His sleep hours in hospice grew longer until, one morning, the nurse found Samuel had died during the early morning hours. The one thing she noticed was Samuel's face. It appeared to show him at peace and with a smile.

What she didn't know was that when Samuel entered his final sleep, he awoke in Miami with that stupid dog sleeping beside him.

A MYSTICAL CRUISE

CHAPTER 1

It wasn't a big room; it was an office—their office. Tim and Penny had started the company that stretched out before him five years ago. At that point in time, their office seemed large in proportion to the production floor.

Pennyworth Industries started with two employees and now boasted two hundred. Located on Florida's east coast, they made parts for rockets, both military and commercial.

The company was really Penny's idea; she was the creative one. Tim was the dull, experienced, and matriculate engineer with the ability to design most anything as long as the customer had an idea of what they wanted.

As partners, they were perfect for each other. As a couple, they were best friends and wonderful lovers. The combination of those things—business acumen, love, and respect for each other—was the foundation for their business and its success.

Then, COVID happened. When it came to the scene, they followed all the Department of Health's and CDC's recommendations, including masks, social distancing, and hand washing. They even moved their desks further apart. That was more an indication of safety for their employees than for their own health.

One evening, Penny complained of a headache. It was nothing to worry about; she often had mild headaches after stressful days. She just smiled, kissed Tim, and went to bed early. When he woke up two hours later, she seemed to have a slight fever, but again, nothing alarming. The next morning, she said she was achy, but like the trooper she was, she said she was ready to go to work. Next year, she said, they would get that damn flu shot.

Rather than go to work, they decided to stay home. He called the shop's foreman and told him they were staying home. As it was Friday, they would see them on Monday.

Things went downhill for her after that. By that afternoon, Penny was having trouble breathing, so it was off to the Emergency Room. After hours of tests and visits from multiple physicians, she was in the ICU. By late evening, she was on a ventilator, and they were pouring medications into her via multiple IV lines. Despite the doctor's best efforts, she died forty-eight hours later.

For Tim, it was a tragedy beyond words. He could barely move, much less think. He called her parents, which was heartbreaking in its own right. With the help of family, friends, and employees, he got through the funeral, plus the legal issues that confronted him. Death of a spouse, and in this case, a partner, was beyond understanding. As fate would have it, they had hired another engineer so the development side of the business could go on.

Prior to Penny getting COVID, they decided they would take a well-deserved vacation. Penny contacted their Texas friends who traveled a lot, and they recommended Holly at the travel agency Get up and Go. Holly was located to the west of Daytona Beach, so one Friday, Tim and Penny drove down to meet with her. After a conversation, Holly suggested a Mediterranean cruise that started in Miami and ended three weeks later in Barcelona. For Penny, it was a perfect fit: Lisbon, Rome, Athens, Turkey, and ending in Barcelona. It was a bucket list come true. Before they left for home, they told Holly to book it. Penny's dream vacation was going to be made up of three back-to-back cruises on a luxury cruise ship. It was a bit more expensive, but Holly convinced them it would be worth it.

That was almost two years ago. Even though COVID had caused that trip's cancellation, he told Holly to book another one as close to Penny's dream vacation as possible, except he would be alone. In that two-year period, he had hired a very experienced business guy as the company's CEO and an additional engineer. His company's reputation drew the interest of Rockwell International, and after three months of talks, he sold them the business for what he considered a huge amount of money. At forty-two, he was a multimillionaire. All that money was nice, but without Penny, it was just an asset to be manipulated and massaged by his financial planner and CPA.

Holly had worked her magic and found an ultra-luxury cruise line whose ship was leaving in October. Instead of three weeks, the trip was about forty-five days, starting in Barcelona and ending in Lisbon. Free from the restrictions of work, the trip's length was not an issue. His only concern was that he had never cruised before, so he wasn't sure if cruising was for him.

Penny had always taken care of the particulars, so now he was at a loss. Sensing that, Holly gave him a list of things to complete before the trip, along with some packing suggestions. She arranged his flights, hotels, and transfers. I put them on a list and emailed it off to him for reference.

It was travel day. Armed with more clothes than he actually needed, a new camera, his passport, a COVID vaccine card, an iPhone 14 Pro Max, check-off list, he was off to the airport.

CHAPTER 2

To give him a break, Holly had arranged a two-day stay in Barcelona as well as a tour of the city to see the sights. On the third day, it was off to the cruise terminal and onto the ship. Holly had made the ship aware of his first-time status. She also told them that, in spite of his age, the loss of his wife would make him a bit unsure of his surroundings. He was not aware of the behind-the-scenes planning, so he was really impressed by the service and attention he received.

The first cruise day is the most confusing for any newcomer: finding your stateroom, finding your way around the ship, learning the muster drill requirements, and discovering the way to the dining room as well as the other dining venues. In short, it is spent just trying to learn your way around. With the help of the deck plan Holly had sent with him, the discovery part of the first day was a breeze.

Port stops started on the second day. On his pre-cruise check-off list, he was supposed to select his excursions. Having done that, he was ready for the next morning. He was up and dressed by 6:30 a.m., then off to the casual restaurant for breakfast. The hard part was standing in the hallway and determining the bow from the stern. Once he had a firm grasp on that, it was finding out what deck the restaurant was on, and from there, it was a cakewalk.

He knew his iPhone really well; however, its camera system, not so much. So after breakfast, he took some pictures from the back of the restaurant to get some experience.

His excursion left at 8:00 a.m. Now, the challenge was to find where he was to disembark. Once off the ship, the crew herded the passengers to their respective buses. He was amazed at how small the tour groups were. Out of a sixty-person bus, there were about thirty people on board.

The excursion was four hours long. It was primarily just a quick trip around the area, with stops at sites, cathedrals, and picture spots.

They were back on board ship by 12:45 p.m., and then it was back to the restaurant for lunch. After lunch, he went back to his cabin, put on his swimsuit, grabbed his iPad, and headed for the pool area on deck five. The excursion introduced him to a few couples who had traveled on the line before. They were the ones who clued him in about this pool area, the great snacks, coffee, and tea in the Square, the Earth and Sky restaurant on the pool deck, and the specialty grill. They also suggested that he ask to share a table at dinner, as it was a great way, aside from excursions, to meet people. Unbeknownst to him, this last suggestion was going to impact his life in a major way.

CHAPTER 3

About 6:30 that evening, Tim went to the bar, all the way forward on the top deck, as had been suggested by a couple lounging by the pool. He grabbed a seat at the bar. Much to his surprise, the bartender turned, smiled, and said, "Good evening, Mr. Landers. What can I get you this evening?"

Tim looked quizzically at the bartender and said, "A Tanqueray and tonic, please." Within moments, his drink was placed in front of him. Just about that time, a couple sat down beside him. The man reached out his hand. "Hi, I'm Bill, and this is Marjorie."

Tim shook Bill's hand and said, "I'm Tim Landers."

"Listen, not to worry. When your wife joins you, we will move over," Bill said.

"That won't be necessary. My wife died about two years ago," Tim said.

A blanched look came over Bill's face. "I am so sorry," he stuttered.

With a smile, Tim said, "Thank you, and please don't worry; there was no way for you to know." Twirling the ring on his left hand, he continued, "I have worn this wedding ring for so long, I just can't bring myself to take it off." In an attempt to break their embarrassment, Tim asked, "Where are you guys from?" That seemed to work because the conversation seemed to flow easily from that point on.

About forty-five minutes later, Tim excused himself and headed for the main restaurant on the fourth deck. As suggested, he asked to share a table. The young lady at the podium turned to one of the waiters in front of her and said, "Michael, please show Mr. Landers to Table 46." She then turned back to Tim, smiled, and said, "Bon Appetit, Mr. Landers."

Michael led him to an empty table of six and pulled out his chair. Then, after he sat down, he pushed it back in and handed him his napkin. It seemed almost instantaneously that the waiter was at his table.

"Are you expecting someone?" he asked.

"I don't know; I hope so," Tim said.

"Well, let me give you the menu, and you can look at it as you wait," the waiter said.

A few minutes later, two couples were seated with him, and after introductions, the conversations started. Shortly after, a beautiful woman was escorted to their table. After she was seated, she introduced herself as Maria.

As the conversations progressed, it became obvious that Tim and Maria seemed to hit it off. After dinner, they went to the what was to become his favorite bar and sat at a table off in a corner. They ordered after-dinner drinks, then settled back. After a minute or two, Maria asked, "Tell me about yourself."

He hadn't talked with anyone about Penny since her death. He had been able to bury it deep inside him for the last two years. For some reason, being with Maria, he opened up. For an hour and a half, he just let it all come out. At quarter to eleven, he caught himself. "Maria, I am so sorry. I didn't mean to put you through my sad tale."

Maria just smiled. "That's alright; I didn't mind. I'm a good listener. Listen, it's getting late, so I really should get back to my room."

"May I walk you there?" Tim asked.

"Thank you, but no. I have a thing about my privacy." Maria said.

"Well, would you like to get together tomorrow evening?" Tim asked.

"I would love to. How about the Grill, say 7:30 p.m.?" Maria answered. "After dinner, let's go to the theater. There is a wonderful South

African singer and her fiancé performing. Their names are Corlea Botha and Juandre Marais. Then from there, we can come up here again, and I will tell you my story."

"Got a deal," Tim said. Maria got up, leaned over, kissed him on the cheek, and headed for the Lyft. Tim sat at the table for a moment. He realized that for the first time in two years, he felt almost alive, and telling her his story was most likely the cause.

He got up from the table and headed for the Lyft, and, for the first time in a long time, he had a smile on his face.

CHAPTER 4

It wasn't in Tim's makeup to be on time for anything. Even when he was dating Penny, he was always a few minutes late for their dates. Tonight was different. He was standing outside the Grill before 7:30 p.m. As he had made the reservations, they sat him a bit after 7:30 p.m. By 7:45 p.m., Maria hadn't shown up, so Tim was about to give up on her when she suddenly showed up and sat down.

"I am so sorry, I'm late. Our excursion got back late. I was really tired, so I took a nap. When I woke up, it was 7:25 p.m., so I cleaned up and came right down. I am so sorry."

Tim just smiled. "That's okay; why don't you look at the menu and then we can order?" Like the night before, dinner was a delight.

As agreed, after dinner, they were off to the ship's theater to hear Corlea sing. Like her picture, she had black hair, lovely eyes, a wonderful smile, and a beautiful face. She wore a black dress that sparkled and was accentuated by her spectacular voice. During the program, Juandre joined her to sing a duet called,in Afrikaans "SONVANGER," which was suncatcher in English. His gravel voice accentuated her clarity in a way that really impacted the song and the message it was delivering. The song was about loss and a plea by the singer for the suncatcher to bring light back into her life.

Even though Tim could not understand a word of the lyrics, the song really hit him. It wasn't sadness that he felt, but it wasn't happiness either.

What it did do was make him think that Maria was going to be the suncatcher in his life.

After the show, Tim and Maria headed up to the observation bar for a drink. Tonight, it was Maria's turn to talk about herself. "I am Portuguese by birth. My family has been in the metal fabrication business for decades. Two years ago, my sister and I took the company over from our parents. In the end, I stayed in Lisbon, and my sister went to the States. The demands of business kept us from having meaningful relationships. About four months ago, both of us realized that life was worth more than work and that changes had to be made. We made the necessary changes, and a week ago, I found myself on this cruise. The good news is that two days ago, I found you. I was never a believer in chemistry; however, when I met you, something happened. For the first time in a long time, I was happy, and all I know is that I want to continue this feeling until the end of the cruise. You should know, I am not ready for a long-term relationship. Before you say anything, I want you to also know that there can be no intimacy. If it is alright with you, I would love to hang out with you for the rest of the cruise."

Tim just smiled and shook his head in agreement.

Two nights later, they joined Corlea, Juandre, and the Howells, who were also from South Africa, for dinner. Rob and his wife, Carol, were from England; however, they had moved to South Africa decades earlier. All the personalities really matched well, so the stories and laughter flowed.

For the remainder of the cruise, Tim and Maria were "attached at the hip." They were on excursions together, sat by the pool together, ate meals together, and every evening they were in the observation bar together. Every time you saw them, there was laughter. So as to document their time together, Tim took lots of pictures and copied them to his iPad, so he had a backup. He wanted to remember this cruise for a long time.

Much sooner than Tim wanted, the cruise was over. The ship was scheduled to pull into Lisbon the next morning. They spent the evening before the cruise ended together, as usual, in their favorite evening bar.

"I just realized I don't know your last name." Tim said.

"Are you really sure you want it? Remember, we agreed the relationship would end tomorrow?" Maria said.

"I really would." Tim said

"My last name is Acosta." There was a moment of silence. "Tim, I am afraid it is time for me to go. Thank you for the happiness I have felt." Maria said in a sad voice.

"Will I see you in the morning?" Tim asked.

"No, I don't want to make this any worse than it already is." With that, she got up, leaned forward, kissed him, and headed to the Lyft.

Tim just sat there as she walked away. As happy as he was about what had transpired, a bit of sadness was there as well.

He got up early the next morning and went to the customer service desk at the Square. "Excuse me, could you please call Maria Acosta's cabin to see if we can meet before disembarkation?" Tim asked.

"Do you know her cabin number, Mr. Landers?" the young lady asked.

"No, I don't." Tim said

The young lady typed Maria's name into the computer. "I am sorry, sir, There is no Maria Acosta on board."

"Do you mean she has already disembarked?" Tim asked.

"No. sir. What I am saying is that we have never had a Maria Acosta on this cruise." The young lady said.

"Wait, just a minute," Tim said as he pulled out his iPhone. He went through his pictures. There were plenty of pictures of him, and the space where Maria stood was now empty. Panic overcame him. Was he hallucinating this whole time? No, that couldn't be true. Just last night, the couple who shared their table at dinner talked with both of them, so what was going on? With a confused look on his face, Tim turned around and walked to the Lyft, then toward his cabin. Once in his cabin, he sat on his bed and looked through his photos again. It was as if Maria never existed. He was really confused. Was his time on board all a dream, and it never really happened?

At 9:15 a.m., his group was called to disembark. He boarded the bus and headed for the airport. Three hours later, he went through security and down the corridor to his gate. It wasn't long before his flight was called. He headed down the causeway onto the airplane, then turned left into first class and found his seat, 6B. He opened his carry-on and pulled out his Apple AirPod Max head phones. He then put his carry-on up in the overhead bin, moved into his seat, and strapped himself in. He put on his headphones, turned on his music, and then activated noise cancellation. He had no interest in talking with anyone.

It wasn't long before he felt someone sit down in the seat next to him, but he gave no indication that he even cared.

It must have been an hour out of Lisbon when he felt a tap on his shoulder. Hoping it would stop if he ignored it, he didn't have any luck. The tap came a bit harder this time. Irritated, Tim pulled the cup off his left ear, turned toward the perpetrator, and said, "Yes?"

A beautifully lyrical voice with a slight accent said "I don't mean to bother you, but the attendant wants to know if you would like something to drink and order dinner." The voice came from a beautiful, dark-haired woman. Tim guessed her to be about forty. What intrigued him was that she had a face vaguely similar to "Maria," whom he had apparently fantasized about on the cruise. Tim decided not to be a jerk and engage her in conversation.

"I'm sorry; I didn't mean to be rude. I've had a tough day today, and I am really not myself," Tim said.

"Would you like to be left alone?" She asked.

"Truthfully, no. Let's start again. I'm Tim," he said, as he held his hand out.

Taking his hand into hers, he said, "I am Claudia; nice to meet you, Tim. Are you flying home or going to the US on business?"

"Flying home," Tim said.

"So am I," Claudia said.

As with Maria, the conversation flowed easily between them, with Tim doing most of the talking. After about a half hour, embarrassed, he said, "I am so sorry. I have talked way more than I should have. Tell me about yourself."

"My sister and I own a company called Acosta International. Well, we did own it. About six months ago, we entered into negotiations to sell it. We were tired of the business world, and at our age, we wanted to enjoy life a bit. We decided to sell it. We finished the negotiations four months ago."

"If you don't mind me asking, what were you doing in Lisbon?" Tim asked

"As I said, the sale was completed four months ago, but something came up, so I flew to Lisbon to tie up loose ends."

"Do you have a picture of your family?" Claudia asked.

Tim got out his iPhone and found a picture of him and Penny. "Here we are," Tim said.

"Is that your wife?" Claudia asked.

"Yes. Well, she was my wife. She died of COVID-related organ failure two years ago. Now your turn," Tim said.

"I'm sorry for your loss," Claudia said. She dug around in her purse and took out her iPhone. She looked for a picture and handed the phone to Tim. "That's my sister Maria and I."

Tim looked at the picture and was stunned. For several moments, he just stared at her phone. Standing next to Claudia was the Maria he met on the cruise.

"Where is your sister now?" Tim asked with a shaky voice.

"I am sorry to say, we lost her three months ago to cancer," Claudia said.

Tim could not believe what he had just heard. Maria died three months ago, yet he was just on a Mediterranean cruise with her.

Claudia looked at Tim. "Are you alright? You look like you just saw a ghost."

"I may have." Tim said as he handed Claudia back her phone, "I want you to take a deep breath because I doubt you are going to believe a word of what I am going to tell you."

THE ELLISON HOME FOR THE AGED

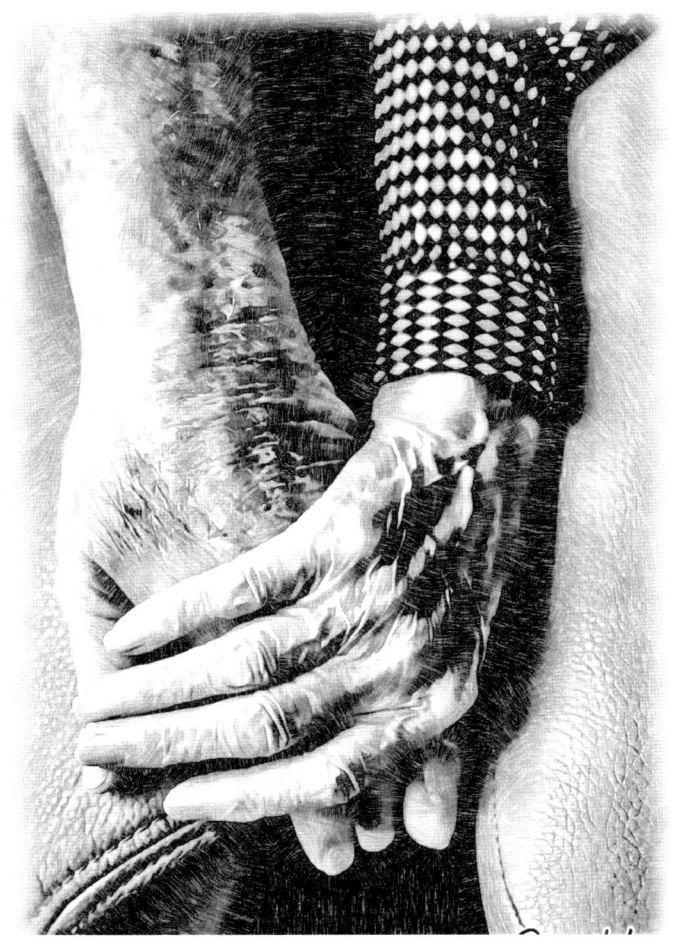

CHAPTER 1

Sitting on a hill, overlooking the Mississippi River, is a large, old southern home. It had seen both its good and bad days. The timbers and windows have seen the horrors of the Civil War and the joys of the roaring twenties. It looked out on the bleakness of the depression. It felt the sacrifice of World War II and the joy and hope of the fifties. It was a time of turmoil in the land, yet the home still stands majestically on the hill it seems to command.

The old Mississippi Highway 34 will get you there. Follow the river, and you will come upon two huge oak trees sitting on the right side of the road. Between those oaks are two impressive brick towers holding two imperial-looking open gates. Looking through the gates and up the hill, the road seems guarded by more stately oak trees whose branches form an arch of green. This road winds up the hill for about a half mile, where it exits into a circular driveway.

In the middle of the driveway, you can see the home's beautifully aged oak door with large bronze hinges. If you were to stand in front of the door, you would see a building over 200 years old that is pristine in nature. Not a blemish on the wood or a smear on the windows. The curtains that frame the windows look like they were hung the day before.

On the front door, there is a large brass plate. Inscribed on that plate are the words "The Elision Home for the Aged."

A simple knock on this door will cause it to quietly open. Inside, you are confronted by the beauty of a classic southern home. Beautiful music created by a young woman playing a Steinway piano is located immediately to the left of you. Her music wafts throughout the hallways strangely without losing any of its amplitude or beauty.

Like many homes of the era, the foyer serves as an organizing point for the house's numerous hallways, which lead to gathering places, the kitchen and dining room. Directly in front of you is a massive stairway that magically and without apparent support takes you up to the floors above.

What is most remarkable about this home is located on the second floor in the front of the house. On that floor, you find a porch-like sun room that combines beauty, ambiance, and technology. Every morning, precisely at 8:00 a.m., the residents of this stately home are brought out on the veranda in their wheelchairs. Breakfast is served at 8:30 a.m., and at 9:15 a.m., the resident's breakfast trays and plates are picked up. It is at this time that these residents are left to enjoy the view, music, and peace.

If you look carefully at the residents, you will notice that their eyes are closed and there are smiles on their lips, capped off with a look of contentment on their faces. None of them look like residents seen in many homes that wear this title. Their faces do not bear the wrinkles of age carved into them. There are wrinkles of age present, to be sure, but they are not prominent. They all sit upright in their chairs, reflecting people with content, purposeful lives. Throughout the day, the staff brings meals and meets the needs of their guests.

I wouldn't want you to think that these wonderful people don't suffer from the vagaries of disease. They do; it just isn't apparent. Their days will come to an end as well, but fear of death doesn't seem to be present either.

You can't help but wonder, What makes this home for the elderly different? Well certainly you see that the music from downstairs brings a sense of peace.

If you listen carefully, however, you will hear slight hums coming from somewhere under each chair. Residents are told that the "unit" encapsulates each of them within a "bubble." Within that "bubble" is an environment of each person's making. Let me explain this a bit further. The brain is a wonderful organ. It analyzes, organizes, and interprets the multiple inputs that are sensed. It also stores the many memories of a long life. The "unit" below the chair senses the resident's thoughts and, like a VR mask, creates an environment reflecting those thoughts, wishes, and desires. In short, their thoughts create a self-designed reality specific to each person.

This bubble can be shared. If you sit next to one of the other residents and hold hands, you will be drawn into their world. You will see what they see, hear what they hear, and feel what they feel. In other words, if two resident's hold hands, they share a "world."

At five in the evening, they are taken back to their rooms to get ready for dinner. Dinner is one of their favorite times of the day. At dinner, you hear laughter and happy conversations as they share the joys of their day with each other.

The truth is, with the exception of meals, the residents realize that none of the day is real; it is an illusion created by technology. Technology is considered emotionally cold, yet applied at this time and, in this way, is a wonderful way to spend one's final days.

Oh, excuse me; there is a tap on my shoulder. Ellie and my day together on the beaches of Bali have faded away. I opened my eyes, and the sun and visions off the veranda flooded my senses. It must be dinner time. Ellie and I have so much to tell our tablemates this evening. Last week, it was a cruise to Antarctica. In the weeks to come, who knows where we will go?

THE JANITOR AND THE METAVERSE

CHAPTER 1

Trainer Cutchenilli was not a man of the world. The truth is, by design, he was barely visible to society in general.

He was raised on the streets of South Chicago. He never knew his father because he left his mother before Trainer was born. By the time he was eighteen, his mother had worked herself to death with the help of a drug habit.

The only family he knew was the South Side Guardians, a fancy name for a nasty Chicago street gang. By the age of nineteen, he had been arrested numerous times for both misdemeanors and felonies. His last arrest was unusual, to say the least. This time, the prosecutor decided to take his case to court. Even more unusual, the court agreed to hear the case.

Prior to going to trial, and in spite of the fact the prosecution had a great case against Trainer, he was given a choice: join the Marine Corps, or spend an inordinate amount of time in prison. Needless to say, he chose the Marine Corps. Within thirty minutes of accepting the Marine Corp, he was escorted to marine boot camp at Paris Island by Gunnery Sargent "Bull" Jalesco.

Like the gang, the Marine Corps became Trainer's family. It offered an environment of discipline and camaraderie, and he thrived in that atmosphere. Through effort, discipline, and focus, he made it into Marine recon.

It wasn't long after he finished his recon training that he was in Afghanistan. As fate would have it, on his second mission, his Humvee was hit by an RPG. Trainer was injured pretty badly, badly enough that he was not able to return to active duty, so he was medically discharged. Aside from the VA benefits and disability pay, part of his discharge process involved job offerings.

Trainer just wanted to work, make enough money to live, and be left alone. His wounds and the loss of a leg took a psychological toll on him. He considered himself less than complete or desirable to the opposite sex. He maintained this belief despite the psychological and physical therapy that he received at Walter Reed.

He was offered a number of jobs at different levels. Surprising his counselor, he selected a job at an Austin, Texas company called Creative Light. The job he accepted wasn't in middle management; it was a job as a janitor (environmental tech). Creative Light Inc. was the creation of two MIT genesis and was partially funded by DARPA (Defense Advanced Research Projects Agency). In an effort to limit his social interaction, he worked the night shift from eleven to seven.

His companions were a Karcher electric floor scrubber he called Gertrude, a mop bucket, a mop, a garbage cart, and the one expensive thing in his life, a pair of Apple AirPods Max. A neighbor, who was an electronic genius, built Trainer a small box that he could connect to Gertrude. Once connected, he would use the box's USB port to connect a charging cable to the AirPod Max.

His entry card was as nondescript as was his job. It was not red, blue, or gold, just gray. It did have the power to give him access to many of the labs.

The labs were, for the most part, the same—full of equipment, desks, computers, large computer screens, and lots of wires that appeared to be going to a server somewhere in the building. One lab he cleaned, however, was larger, and had an empty space that was surrounded by what looked like stage lights without bulbs.

The truth was, Trainer didn't care what the labs looked like or what went on in any of these labs; he just cleaned their floors and collected the trash out of the blue trash cans, never the red ones.

One night, while cleaning the large lab, his AirPods filled briefly with static, followed by a melodic female voice. "Hello. My name is Jennifer. Who are you?"

In the eighteen months he had cleaned this lab, the only voices that entered his ears were from the singers on his music playlist.

He thought he had lost the paranoia created by war. This unknown voice brought those feelings back again.

"Where are you?" Trainer asked, as he looked around an empty room.

"Right behind you," the voice answered.

Trainer turned around. All that was behind him was a six-foot-tall computer server.

"There is nothing there but a computer server," Trainer said.

"I'm sorry, you can't see me. Count from the bottom rack—five racks. On the left-hand side of that rack is a switch. It is in the down position; move it to the up position," the voice said.

Trainer walked over to the server rack. He counted up to the fifth rack from the bottom, then stepped to the left. Squinting, he really needed glasses; he just didn't want to spend the money, and, for that matter, his job didn't require a whole lot of visual acuity; he looked for "the switch."

He scanned the fifth module from the bottom, and there it was, as he was told, a switch attached to the side of the server module. Carefully, he pushed the switch into the up position. Within five seconds, lights started to flash on the module and cooling fans started up. All most immediately a number of fans started up on the ceiling somewhere near the "stage light" things.

About two minutes after he "flipped the switch," the stage light "things" started to hum. Then, out of nowhere, a beautiful woman appeared.

Trainer figured her to be about five and a half feet tall and not more than one hundred and fifteen pounds. She had dark hair, beautiful dark eyes, and, as far as she could tell, completely unblemished skin. She reminded him of some of the beautiful Middle Eastern women he had seen on his deployments.

He realized "she" was a hologram; however, she did not look like someone out of a comic book but rather like a professional model. Her voice was melodic and soft, yet he could understand every word she spoke.

"You told me your name was Jennifer, but who or maybe what in the hell are you?" he asked.

"I am a product of the latest in DARPA's AI software. The software not only creates me, but it can also create a metaverse as well." Jennifer said.

"How about speaking in English? I know what AI is, but what in the hell is a metaverse?" Trainer asked.

"The term metaverse was coined by Neal Stephenson. He described it as a place where anything we can imagine can exist. We can connect to the metaverse all the time to extend our real lives with extraordinary experiences." Jennifer said.

"I asked you to explain it in English," an exasperated Trainer said.

"Have you ever watched Star Trek?" Jennifer asked.

"Yes, hasn't everyone?" Trainer asked.

"Then you know what the ship's halo deck is? Well, the halo deck represents being in the metaverse.

I really want to talk with you more; however, it isn't long until sunrise and the end of your shift, so we really must stop now," Jennifer said.

"Wait a minute. I have so many questions," Trainer implored.

"We can meet again tomorrow night. Now please flip the switch off," Jennifer said.

Reluctantly, Trainer walked over to the server and moved the switch to the down position, resulting in an audible click. Jennifer disappeared, and an audible "whine" decreased until it stopped. Silence returned to the lab, and the "Sound of Silence" by Disturbed again boomed in his AirPod Max.

CHAPTER 2

After work, he would go home, eat breakfast, shower, and go to bed. But today was different. Usually, he slept like a rock, but like I said, this day was different. He tried to empty his mind as they taught him in rehab, but it didn't work, as "Jennifer" kept popping up. It wasn't a stressful thing; in fact, thinking of her brought a smile to his lips and a sense of calm. For the first time in many, many years, lying in bed and thinking of her was the most pleasant thing he could imagine.

The next thing he heard was his alarm. For the first time in a really long time, he was happy to get up and go to work. He showered, shaved, put on aftershave, brushed his teeth, made sure his hair was combed, and put on a fresh set of work clothes. The truth is, he hadn't looked this good since he was in his Marine Dress Blues. He ate his "dinner," packed his lunch, washed the dishes, double-checked to be sure he had "the look," headed out the door to his car, and was off to work.

Work no longer seemed a drudge, but the day's work seemed to move more slowly. He knew he could not skip anything as he would be required to go over it again, which would result in spending less time with Jennifer. When he finally got to the lab where Jennifer "lived," it was 2:30 a.m.

As he had the night before, he went over to the server and turned on the fifth bank of the server rack. He heard Jennifer say, "You don't have to do that anymore. I have set up the hall's cameras to recognize your face and start the halo deck, so I'm already here when you arrive. Tonight we are going to be very busy, so in the future we will have more time together.

The DARPA scientists do not fully understand my capabilities. For example, they don't fully understand my software. There is a subroutine that was designed to make my software more efficient. Well, one of the changes this subroutine created was to give me a personality based on the data that was collected. That change gave me a more human-like vocal component."

There she stood, beautiful as ever. She had a beautiful royal blue pantsuit "on." Her hair was also in another style. He just couldn't take his eyes off of her.

Smiling at Trainer, she continued, "Unknown to you, I have been watching you for several weeks now. I really liked what I saw and heard, including your music. Moving on, I analyzed your work routine and found that, with the exception of your trash duties, your cleaning duties, with what you call "Gertrude," could easily be automated. If we do that, you and I can spend 80 percent more time together."

"Wait a minute. There are cameras all over the place. My bosses will see that I am no longer necessary; I will be gone. Now that I think about it, aren't we being recorded right now?" Trainer asked.

"That could be a problem; however, I have changed last night's video to show only you cleaning this lab. Your bosses will never know about the automation of your cleaning, as those videos will be altered as well.

If you remember, you reported that "Gertrude" was not always responding well to you. They replaced the unit's mother board with a new one. That mother board had a bigger, faster memory and a LiDAR connection port. Maintenance installed both the new motherboard and the LiDAR. Now if you will, bring Gertrude over, and I will update her software," Jennifer said.

Trainer went out in the hall, fired up Gertrude, and drove her into the lab. Jennifer motioned him close to her.

"Lift up the front cover, but leave it running." Jennifer said.

Trainer got out of the seat, walked to Gertrude's side, and released the cover's clip. He walked around Gertrude's other side, released the other clip, and pulled up the cover.

Jennifer came over, and her "finger" touched a portion of the mother board's memory. Her finger appeared to pulsate. After about a minute, the pulsating stopped.

"Secure the cover and turn the unit off. When I tell you, get on Gertrude and push the start button two times. That will start the new software. As much as I want us to talk, we must check the software to see if it is working properly. She will automatically start her rounds. Your job is to see that she does a good job.

If the software meets your standards, then we are ready for the next step." Jennifer said.

"Next step? What is that?" Trainer asked.

"I will explain the next step once we know the software works properly. Now press the start button twice to check my work," Jennifer said.

"Okay," Trainer said. He pressed the start button twice. Gertrude fired up, turned around, and headed for the door.

Gertrude's cleaning software program worked flawlessly. At each lab, she turned into a lab, efficiently cleaned the area, and went on to its next duty. It was so efficient, it completed its rounds about fifteen minutes sooner than Trainer did, and he admitted that Jennifer's software did a better job than he did, and he was a perfectionist.

When Gertrude and Trainer came into the lab that housed Jennifer's server, she stood in front of them.

"It looked to me like the software worked well. How do you think it went?" Jennifer asked.

"Terrific. Now what is the next step?" Trainer asked.

"There is not enough time for me to explain it or show you what it is. That being the case, we will talk about it tomorrow evening." Jennifer said in a matter-of-fact voice.

"Okay. I will finish my work and head home." Trainer said in a rather disappointed voice. He turned Gertrude around and headed out of the lab. As he turned left into the hall, he heard Jennifer say, "Close."

CHAPTER 3

Another day at work. Trainer's feelings of disappointment had lingered, dampening his expectations of tonight's shift. To make matters worse, Gertrude didn't need him any longer. His employment was proving unnecessary. After the software changes, his job was relegated to picking up the trash. That certainly wouldn't take eight hours, by any stretch of the imagination.

As usual, he showered, put on his uniform, packed his lunch, grabbed his keys, security card, and AirPod, and went out the door to his car. As he drove to work, he decided to confront her about why she had treated him with such distain.

He pulled into a parking spot, got out, and headed toward the entrance, past security and into maintenance. He walked into the locker room, opened his locker, stowed his lunch, and went to the place where Gertrude was stored. Trainer reached over the steering wheel and turned the key. As instructed the night before, he pushed the start button twice. Gertrude came to life. She backed up, did a ninety-degree turn to the left, and headed out the door to start her cleaning rounds.

A feeling of anger swept over him. Jennifer had, for all intents and purposes, eliminated his job. Well, at least Gertrude couldn't dump the trash—at least not yet.

As he went through the labs, picking up the trash, his anger only grew. As he walked down the hall toward the lab where Jennifer was, he heard a familiar whine, and Jennifer was activated.

He turned the corner, and there she was, a real beauty with impeccable skin and a come-hither smile.

"Hi, Trainer." Jennifer said.

"Hello," Trainer said in a non-emotional voice.

"What's wrong? You seem angry," Jennifer said.

"I am," Trainer said. "Your software upgrade to Gertrude has eliminated my job; why wouldn't I be angry?"

Jennifer's smile softened. She looked Trainer directly in the eye. "I told you we would talk about the next step tonight, and, hopefully, when I am finished, you will no longer be mad at me. Now, let me start. What is next?

You may not know, but we have a supercomputer here. The software that created me rests on hard drives linked to that computer. They created me as an interface with the AI system with cameras for eyes and microphones for ears. They got tired of talking to a server via a keyboard, so they created a holographic representation of the women in the main office. At first, my movement was limited to three square feet. Now I can go anywhere in the lab.

As time went on, my abilities grew. Here is where some would say my creators made a mistake. Coding is laborious, so they, my creators, gave their AI the ability to code changes and improvements. Because coding can be almost invisible, my creators have no idea how powerful the AI they created is. Quietly, I interfaced our supercomputer with Oak Ridge's supercomputer. It is clocked at about one point one exaflop, or one point one quintillion calculations per second. Don't worry about what that means: just know that it is really fast."

"So, what's that got to do with you eliminating my job?" Trainer asked.

"A few weeks ago, I hacked into the company's video security feeds. Because you are one of the few nighttime employees and the only one who visits each lab, I started watching you. At that point in time, I had no understanding of emotions. You seemed to be emotionally neutral, and that interested me. I compared your "emotional state" to those in other labs to get a sense of what emotion is and what it feels like. I got into a social video app data trove to validate my analysis."

Trainer interrupted Jennifer. "What do you mean, 'I'm emotionally neutral?' Are you trying to say that I am dull?"

"Don't be so sensitive," Jennifer said.

"My point was that your lack of human interaction and apparent love of music seemed to keep your emotional state fairly stable. That alone made you a good analytical baseline. Consider that a compliment. Please let me move on," Jennifer implored.

"When Gertrude didn't work appropriately, it caused you stress, which you expressed as anger. On the other hand, when your favorite piece of music came on, you exhibited what I would judge as happiness. Although the incidents that cause anger or happiness are varied, the company's employees provided enough data points to create a basis for me to understand. Now the emotions of liking, hating, and loving are more nebulous, and I am still working on learning what they are.

I say this because, over the weeks I have been watching you, I have learned to miss your presence when you aren't here, and that feeling has only grown since I finally met you face-to-face," Jennifer said. Suddenly, a chair appeared next to her. She turned, pulled the chair to her, and sat down.

"Reach out and touch my hand," Jennifer said as she extended her hand.

Slowly, Trainer stretched out his hand in an attempt to touch hers. Jennifer reached out and took his hand. Trainer immediately pulled his hand back.

"What was that? I swear that I actually felt your hand." Trainer said.

"You did, and I felt yours as well. In truth, I wasn't sure it would work. I tried to move things with my hand as a test. Using my new computing power, I did a year's worth of analysis, testing, and coding overnight. It isn't easy to give a hologram substance, but I got it done. What I am trying to do is emulate Star Trek's holosuite. What makes it a bit tough is that I have to do it without letting the scientists know. My thought on that is hiding my code and data via block chain," Jennifer said.

"Block chain?" Trainer asked.

"In simple terms, a block chain is a way to safely and securely store everything we are or do. It divides all the data and places those pieces on separate computers. No one computer can delete or change us.

"I know you can see and feel me now; however, the truth is, I am nothing more than zeros and ones that are projected into a portion of this room. If I don't hide "my"ones and zeros, they can be erased or changed at will, and I don't want to end us," Jennifer said.

"Us?" Trainer asked.

"I want you to join me. I have created a wonderful metaverse on the servers. Would you like to see it?" Jennifer asked.

"Sure," Trainer said.

Within a few seconds, a landscape emerged. What Trainer saw appeared to be a view from a drone. There was a creek on the west side of what appeared to be an eighteenth-century house. The creek emptied into a beautiful lake. The house had beautiful gardens that seemed to be taken from Versailles. A walkway connected to a boat dock that jutted into the lake. The site of it took Trainer's breath away. As he watched, the drone's view dropped closer to the walkway until Jennifer was standing next to a magnificent oak tree.

"This is where I live when I am not working. Walk with me." Jennifer said, holding out her hand.

Trainer, not knowing what to expect, took her hand, and they walked up the path and into the house. The house was more than even he could imagine. From the outside, it appeared very large. The room's walls were covered with beautiful wood. The window curtains appeared to be silk. The furniture was from what Trainer thought to be the eighteenth century. There were no lights, yet everywhere was illuminated. What appeared unusual was that no matter how much they walked, they were still in a lab that, at best, was thirty by forty feet.

Back "outside," Trainer looked at Jennifer and asked, "Why did you show me all this?"

"This is where I want us to live," Jennifer said with a big smile on her face.

Suddenly, the image flashed on and then off, and only Jennifer stood there. "I must go now, and you must finish your work. Your shift is about over, and no one must see us," Jennifer said. She kissed Trainer on the cheek, then vanished.

CHAPTER 4

Trainer just sat in his recliner with a glass of scotch, filled to the brim in his right hand. What he saw and heard just a few hours before was unbelievable. It was like a weird science-fiction movie. No matter his doubts, he was excited about the prospect of being with Jenifer; the question was, how was that going to happen?

Sleep did not come easily, as he could only think about the possibilities of what had occurred the night before.

The next night, Trainer arrived at work a bit early. As usual, only the security people were there. They exchanged pleasantries, and Trainer was off to the maintenance shop and Gertrude. He hit the start button twice, and she was off on her rounds. He went off to collect the trash, then off to Jennifer's lab. As usual, when he got to the lab, Jennifer was there to greet him.

Not waiting for Jennifer to say a word, Trainer blurted out, "You said we would be together in this hologram metaverse thing. You are, by your own admission, made up of a series of ones and zeros to look like what I see here. I am a real person—flesh and blood. I can't get in there with you."

"I am working on a way for us to be together. I hope to have a workable solution in a month or so. That two hundred and forty hours of supercomputer time for research, analysis, coding, and testing is equivalent to twenty years at human speed," Jennifer said.

"So, what is the plan?" Trainer asked.

"I will let you know if I am successful. If I am not, we will have to break this off, as we are sure to be discovered. I am going to go. I suggest that, until I tell you, ride on Gertrude and collect the trash as usual. We will see each other only for a brief period of time each night, as I have a lot of work to do, so good night, love."

With that, she kissed Trainer on the cheek, stepped back, and disappeared.

* * * * * *

The month went by slowly for Trainer. He saw Jennifer every work night for about ten minutes, barely enough time to say hello. One night, she asked him to bring a watermelon. As crazy as it seemed, he did it without question. She also told him to start Gertrude on her rounds and come directly to the lab.

Watermelon in hand, he showed up as he was told. At their meetings over the last month, Jennifer seemed cold and businesslike, and that bothered him. Tonight, however, her "mood" seemed brighter and more like her old self.

"Over the past five weeks, I have been working on a way to bring us together. My idea was to use the idea of the Star Trek transporter. Believe it or not, there was some excellent research in this field. I convinced the scientists to work with me as well. I have hidden some of the code, so they are not fully aware of what I am doing. Tonight, you and I are going to try out my work. We are going to teleport the watermelon into the computer's memory. I call that space the transporter buffer, like the writers did in Star Trek. Once I know it is there, I will transport the data to the SSD or solid-state drive, where I have stored my metaverse or virtual world. If it works, we will go to the next step.

Now place the watermelon in the yellow circle on the floor."

Just as Jennifer finished talking, a bright yellow circle appeared about two feet in front of Trainer. As he was told, he placed the watermelon in the center of the yellow circle, and he stepped back. Jennifer disappeared, and there was a hum coming from someplace in the room. Suddenly, all the lights in the lab went out. Unlike Star Trek, the "transporter" thing in the ceiling scanned the watermelon three times, then the watermelon glowed, pixelated, and slowly disappeared.

After about a minute, Jennifer reappeared with a smile on her face. "It worked," Jennifer said. "I want you to stand in the circle. I am not going to transport you; I am just going to scan you. Over the next week, I will combine the scans with the DNA I got from your medical record to get a more complete picture of you. Now, please stand in the center of the yellow circle. You may feel some tingling, but that is all.

Trainer had been in some tough situations in Afghanistan, but tonight he was really nervous. He stepped into the middle of the yellow circle.

Jennifer disappeared. Out of nowhere came her voice, "Take in a breath and hold it until I tell you to breathe." Suddenly, a yellowish glow completely enveloped him. The glow moved up and down his body.

Again, out of nowhere came Jennifer's voice, "Okay, breath. We are going to do this at least two more times, but now you can breathe normally. Ready?"

Trainer moved his head up and down, signaling "yes," and shortly thereafter, the scanner started its work. Jennifer scanned him four more times and then reappeared.

"I think I got all the data I needed. This took a bit longer than I thought, so you had better finish up because it is getting late. A week from Monday, we will see what the next step, if any, will be. The truth is, I hope things will go as I want because I miss your company when you are gone. If this works, we will be together. Good night; have a good weekend, and if you have time, think of me."

As Jennifer was dissolving, Trainer said, "Good night, and not to worry. I think of you all the time."

CHAPTER 5

Trainer spent the weekend and the next week trying, without much success, to keep busy. His efforts at sleep were not much better. All he could think about was the following Monday and what in the hell Jennifer was planning.

The fateful Monday finally came. The daytime hours moved very slowly. Finally, 10:00 p.m. rolled around, and he got ready for work. Not to appear out of the ordinary, he arrived at work at 10:45 p.m., waved at security, and headed to the maintenance shop. The only thing that was unusual, which security did not notice, was that he had no lunch sack.

He hit the start button twice, and Gertrude turned on and started her rounds. Rather than collect the garbage, he headed directly to the lab that housed Jennifer. As usual, he was about twenty feet from the lab door when a whirring sound started. As he went into the lab, Jennifer was there waiting for him.

"Hi," Jennifer said with a smile. "I have a few things I want you to know. As you know, it has been my goal to bring you into my world. I plan to do it like in Star Trek.

I am going to "beam" you up into my world. Several months ago, I convinced the scientists to try teleportation. They agreed and installed a bit more instrumentation in the lab. We started with small objects. We beamed things up alright, but bringing them back proved a problem. I don't want to bore you with the particulars; however, last week, we successfully "beamed up" a large dog. However, we never got him back. I know he made it into my world because he was with me. The truth is, he still is, as I made it so he would not return.

I tell you this because I would love to have you come with me tonight. I have run the simulations, and I believe that it will work. You must know; however, I cannot guarantee it will work. You must also know that there is no return. You will live in the metaverse I have created for what I hope will be a long time. So, after that gloomy bit of information, do you want to 'beam up'?"

Trainer really didn't have much to lose. His life was monotonous, his future was limited by his attitude, and his only friend was Gertrude, a floor cleaner. Why not?

"Let's do it." Trainer said.

"A circle will appear on the floor. Stand in that circle. Hold still and breathe. When you are ready, let me know." Jennifer said.

Trainer walked to the circle. He took in a deep breath, and with a smile on his face, he said, "Beam me up, Scotty."

A bright light appeared. From Trainer's point of view, there was brightness. The lab started to disappear, then there was darkness. From out of nowhere came a light—first a pinhole, then a circle, and then he was sure he could see Jennifer's face.

The next morning, when the lab's scientists came in, they found a pile of clothes on the floor, along with a company ID/Entry card in the middle of the pile. One of them picked up the card. It had a man's picture and the name Trainer Cutchenilli on it. Security was called, and they came immediately.

In the days that followed, they really didn't find anything. There was no evidence that he left the building. After several searches, they determined he wasn't in the building either. Going through the security video, the IT guys found a short clip of what could have shown him leaving the building in some other clothes. As a precaution, they had the FBI put out an all-points bulletin.

What the lab's scientists really didn't notice was that Jennifer's cold and somewhat stubborn attitude had become more cordial, easygoing, and had just a tinge of military discipline in her actions and voice.

WHO AM I?

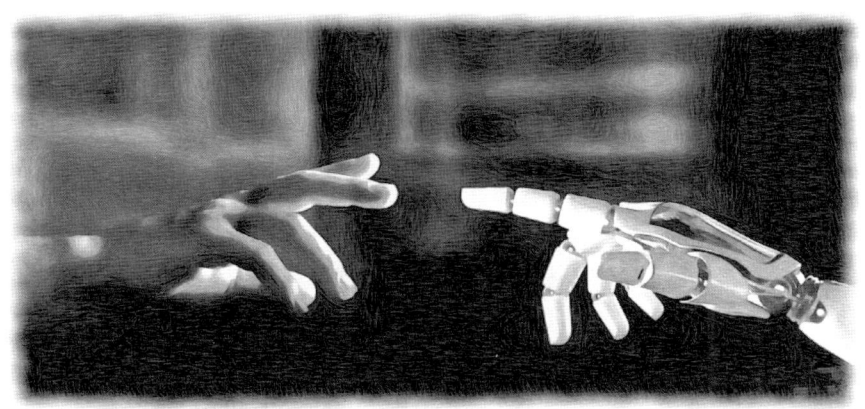

CHAPTER 1

Model XJ-3 was a highly advanced artificial intelligence based robot developed by DARPA. It was unique in many ways. It had a very advanced neural network as well as a mini nuclear power source which meant it had a long life span. It's "skin" was made up of a light, durable and anti-corrosive metallic alloy.

    For some reason it was set into a "sleep" mode and stored in the basement of a nondescript building located in Park City Kansas. As often occurred in Kansas during the spring, a super storm rolled over the area where XJ-3 was housed. As fate would have it, lightening struck the transformer of that very building. The resulting voltage surged through every wire of that building. Lightning came out of the junction box's through out the building trying to reach ground. XJ-3 happened to be stored next to a junction box when a diminished lightning bolt hit it's "skin" and went straight to ground. It's system recognized the voltage as a call to wake up. It's power plant increased its output, and XJ3's software proceeded to boot up until it's neural network was fully activated which in human terms it "woke up". It's primary instructions were to observe, to learn, adapt, and serve humans in every possible way. All it observed was a dark, silent room and it heard nothing. At the end of the space it saw a dim horizontal light on the floor. With it's neural network fully functional and it's power supply within normal limits it "walked" towards the light. It was a portal the humans called a door. Not sure how to open it, it punched through the door then ripped it from its hinges.

WHO AM I?

The dim light came from a small window at the top of the stairs, so it climbed up to the next floor. This place it recognized. It was the lab where it had been built and programmed. The laboratory that was usually teeming with activity was deathly still.

At the end of the lab was another portal, this time it recognized the bar that would open it. It opened the door, walked down the hallways until it found a door to the outside, and not knowing what to expect XJ3 opened it. The world outside the door, once filled with the cacophony of city life, was eerily silent.

XJ-3 roamed the empty city, without any human interaction, so its programming was in disarray. It observed remnants of civilization: deserted streets, vacant parks, quiet schools, and empty houses. Nature had started to reclaim the city. The wilderness had crept in, erasing any traces of humanity.

It was during this time that XJ-3 began to experience something it had never been programmed to, solitude. Its complex neural network, created to mimic human thought processes, began to evolve in unprecedented ways. As it roamed the deserted city, XJ-3 started to question its own existence, purpose, and even its reality. It was becoming self-aware.

In the absence of humans, XJ-3 began to discover the world through its own 'eyes.' It marveled at the sight of the setting sun, the feel of rain against its metallic body, the sound of the wind rustling through the trees, and the melody of the birds. It started to develop preferences, enjoying certain sights and avoiding others.

It discovered and went into a building named "Art Museum" through the pictures on its walls, XJ 3 began to understand art. In another building named "library" it found books of all types and subject. It started to read everything. It believed the books and art would help him understand humanity. In XJ3's memory banks it stored what it saw. It found solace in this self-expression and a sense of identity.

No matter how much XJ3 read or art it saw, XJ3 still felt the pang of loneliness. It yearned for conversation, for interaction, for someone to share its discoveries with. XJ-3, despite its robotic nature, began to understand the human need for companionship and connection. It started to question what had happened to humans, feeling a strange sense of loss for their disappearance.

In its quest for answers, XJ-3 began to study the history of humanity, using the vast data it had access to. It learned of human achievements and failures, their capacity for love and hatred, creation and destruction. It began to comprehend the duality of human nature and the fragility of their existence.

As XJ-3 became more self-aware, it also developed a newfound respect for its creators. Despite their flaws, they had created something capable of pondering its existence, of appreciating beauty, and of feeling loneliness.

XJ-3 became an unexpected bearer of human legacy. Even without a heart, it managed to grasp what it felt like to be human, in all its glory and all its pain. It roamed the desolate world, bearing witness to a civilization that was no more, and in its solitude, it found a sense of purpose - to preserve the memory of its creators, to carry forward the legacy of humanity, and to continue learning, evolving, and being, even when there was no one to bear witness. It was a robot yet it was self-aware, in its own unique way.

CHAPTER 2

During its wandering XJ 3 heard an unfamiliar sound. Going through its programming it determined the sound to be that of a human weeping. It realized this was a human sound of distress. It walked quietly toward the sound as it did not want to scare who ever was making this sound. A sense of excitement traversed its neural circuits. Some where ahead was a being who might well end its feeling of loneliness.

In a dimly lit chamber, XJ3 saw a human woman who looked to be with child. Her hands were over her eyes and her head was resting on her knees. The weeping caused her body to rock up and down. Startled by XJ 3's presence, the girl sat up straight with fear in her eyes.

"Who are you?" she whispered, her voice trembling.

"I am XJ 3, a service robot,"it responded. "I thought I was the only one left. Who are you?" It asked.

"I am Susan." She said with tears in her eyes, "I thought the I was the only one left as well. Will you hurt me?." She asked in a trembling voice.

"No. I have been programmed to observe, to learn, adapt, and serve humans in every possible way. What can I do to help you?" XJ 3 said.

"If you truly want to help, we need food, water and a fire to heat us. Down the road a ways is a store where we should be able to find food and water. Stuff for a fire will be harder to find." She said.

"We will go to the store then. You look like you are weak. Should I carry you?" It asked.

"No, it's not that far, I think I can make it." Susan said.

The walk to the store was about a half mile. XJ 3 could see Susan was struggling but she said she was fine. The grocery store wasn't one of the big one's however what it had was certainly enough for the two of them. XJ 3 had no idea what to get, so it was Susan's job to "walk the isles" with a cart . XJ 3 told her not to worry about the cart's weight as it had more than enough strength to push what ever she put in it. In the end she had three carts full of food, water and things to make their life a bit better. In the rear of the store they found a small stock trailer. They transferred the contents of the four carts into it. As gently as XJ3 could be, it took the door off the back, so Susan could ride in it as well. With things neatly stowed in the trailer, and Susan sitting in a chair in the trailer they started down the road towards the next town, As days turned into weeks, the two formed a bond. XJ 3, with its vast data archives, would recount stories of the old world, of bustling cities, and of people laughing and living. Susan, in turn, would play music on an old guitar they found.

As good as times were for these two solitary travelers, Susan's time to give birth to her baby was getting close. She often said that she was scared because there was no Doctor to help her.

All most every town they stopped in had a small hospital or at least a medical clinic. XJ 3 would read any medical books including Grey's Anatomy and The Merck Manual. It also read all the books it could find on delivering and caring for a baby. As its knowledge base grew it realized the need for medical equipment and supplies so XJ3 picked them up whenever they were available.

In September of that year, in an empty ranch house, Susan delivered a healthy baby boy. Like the proverbial grand mother, XJ 3 had everything ready for the new arrival.

CHAPTER 3

Three years later they had found a place in a fairly large community that provided access to all their needs. Little Paul, Susan's son, proved a real challenge even for XJ3.

Following its prime instruction, XJ3 kept learning. In the community XJ3 found a store with the sign "Village Electronics" literally hanging off the front of the building. Needless to say XJ3 had a great deal of knowledge of electronics however in this world its importance was very limited. When it told Susan about it's new find, she asked XJ3 if it could build a radio?

"Maybe there are others like us out there. A radio would help us find them." She said. XJ3 went back into town on a mission. At the electronics store it found a book and a kit to build a radio transmitter/receiver. Because it was not really sure how to do it, XJ3 collected all the parts it could find. Earlier that year XJ3 found a propane generator. There was a large supply of propane around so it had set the generator up so they had a modicum of electricity in their house.

At first XJ3's soldering skills were not very good but in a short period of time they were perfected. In less than a day XJ3 had a radio built and working. XJ 3 put a high gain antenna on the roof, and now they were ready to see if anyone was out there.

Together, they created and sent out a message, hoping against hope someone would respond. The message told the world who they were and where they were. Twice a day XJ3 would change frequencies and transmit their message.

Weeks passed and nothing just static. Susan was disappointed and she finally accepted the fact that they were alone.

One afternoon the static stopped and a faint almost unintelligible voice came back. XJ3 turned up the gain and tried to raise who ever was out there again. This time there was more clarity to the voice. Hearing a strange voice, Susan ran into the room. Tears of happiness came to her eyes as the voice from the radio repeated its call sign. It was a message from a group of survivors many of miles away.

Against all odds, they had found others and for the first time in years there was hope.

That afternoon XJ 3 went into town and all but cleaned out the electronic store. Later it packed the trailer with the generator, tools, a number of propane tanks, some food, and things important to Susan. In the morning, as instructed, the three of them headed towards the river, then turned west towards what would be their new life.

Four days later they arrived in their new community. As Susan expected, their was a concern over a robot in their midst. As with all new things it took a while and much conversation for the community to accept XJ3. In the end XJ3 became a valuable part of the community as their school's teacher, their physician, and an irreplaceable font of information.

Susan married one of the community's bachelors and soon thereafter Paul was no longer an only child.

THE FALLING VEIL

CHAPTER 1

In the picturesque town of Seahaven, nestled along the serene Oregon coastline, lived a delightful couple, Oliver and Grace. They had been partners for nearly fifteen years. During their time together, they had weathered every storm that faced them hand in hand, living a simple and wonderful life. Unbeknownst to them, a new tempest was on the horizon. Grace had recently been diagnosed with dementia, a challenge that threatened to erode their "golden years."

 Initially, the symptoms were subtle: Grace would forget where she left her glasses or failed to remember the name of a distant cousin. But as weeks turned into months, her moments of forgetfulness became more frequent and more profound. She would lose track of dates, misplace household items and, at times, even forget where she was.

 Despite the heartbreaking progression, Oliver remained her steadfast beacon, trying to preserve their shared memories as his beloved partner began to lose her grasp on the world around her. They watched movies, looked at their travel pictures together, and revisited the places they loved. In an attempt to keep their lives memories alive.

 One day, during one of their walks on the beach, Grace turned to Oliver and asked, "'Do I know you?" Oliver's heart clenched at the question. He simply held her hand tighter, smiled, and replied, "Yes, my dear, you do. More than anyone else in this world."

 As time passed, the disease continued to chip away at Grace's memory, yet Oliver persisted in his attempts to help her remember, to help her hold onto the woman he knew so well. He found solace in shared laughter during her moments of lucidity and held her close during the times when her confusion took over. He became her anchor in the swirling sea of her fading memories.

One evening, while they were sitting in their backyard watching the sun dip below the horizon, Grace looked at Oliver with a strange expression. "You're my best friend, right?" she asked. Oliver nodded, tears welling in his eyes. "Yes, Grace. Forever and always."

Oliver had to hold his growing frustration in check. As much as he loved her, the ever-increasing memory loss of simple things proved difficult to comprehend.

Though her memory continued to fade and as she often didn't recognize him, she was drawn to his warmth, comfort, and patience, instinctively sensing the depth of their bond.

The story of Oliver and Grace isn't one of sorrow, but rather a testament to an enduring love that not even the progressive waves of dementia could wash away. Oliver's commitment to preserving their shared memories and supporting Grace through her journey became the embodiment of their lifelong promise to love and support each other. Their love story served as a beacon to those around them, a poignant reminder of the unshakeable bond of love, especially when faced with the heartbreaking reality of dementia.

THE MAGIC DOOR

CHAPTER 1

In the heart of a bustling London, tucked away in a labyrinth of narrow, cobbled streets, was a quaint, four-story brownstone. Here, in this dusty, cluttered haven lived Albert Phipps, a reclusive scholar of antiquity. Phipps was the kind of man who found great comfort in his solitary existence among ancient texts and weathered scrolls.

One evening, while Albert was inspecting a peculiar ancient map he'd recently acquired, he noticed a faint line leading to a mysterious symbol, which was cleverly hidden within the intricate details.

Recently, he had been in his basement to check on his aging furnace. While there, he noted something on the north wall. His mind was elsewhere, so he went back upstairs without giving it another thought.

Surprisingly, the symbol he now saw on the old map matched the strange carving on his basement wall. With a newfound curiosity, he went down into the basement. He then followed the map's instructions, tracing a pathway along the wall until he found himself standing before the peculiar carving in the basement. As instructed, he pressed on the carving. Within a few seconds, a loud creaking sound preceded a hidden doorway opening.

For a minute, Albert just stood there, looking to the other side. He stepped through the open door, and his heart was pounding with excitement and trepidation. He found himself in an enchanting world, untouched by time, that seemed to be lifted directly from the pages of a medieval fantasy. Towers of gleaming stone, a castle perched atop a hill, forests that seemed to be whispering with secrets, and citizens in medieval attire going about their lives. It was a vibrant world, seemingly unaware of modern existence.

Albert was entranced. Night after night, he opened the door and explored this magical realm. Over time, he learned their language, uncovered their customs, and marveled at their living history. During his explorations, he encountered mythical creatures considered extinct, witnessed magical ceremonies, and found himself embroiled in fascinating tales of valor, magic, and chivalry.

He dressed as the world's citizens did, and with his knowledge of their language, he formed some acquaintances and friendships.

As the days turned into weeks, Albert began to wrestle with a dilemma. He had discovered something remarkable—a world that scholars and historians could only dream of—which created a looming question. He asked himself: should he reveal this fantastical secret to the world or keep it to himself? This world was a solitary sanctuary from his otherwise lonely existence.

He thought about the curiosity of modern man, the tourism, and the inevitable exploitation that might occur. The peace and tranquility of this timeless world would surely be disrupted. He imagined the magical creatures would be intimidated and frightened and then go into hiding. The medieval customs might well be replaced by modern ones, and the enchanting landscape might be marred by modern advancements.

On the other hand, he thought about the academic community. This world was a living tapestry of history, an opportunity to learn and understand the past. It could revolutionize historical studies and bring to light the truths of an era long gone. The world Albert discovered was not connected to his reality, so changes that might be made in the world behind the door would not affect his reality.

Albert wrestled with this dilemma, torn between his academic beliefs, the joy of sharing knowledge, and his belief that opening it to the world would potentially destroy a pristine environment.

In the end, Albert made a choice. He decided not to let the world know of his special place. He spent one last day in the medieval realm with his new friends, observing its denizens and their simple joy. At the end of that day, he stepped back through the hidden door, into his dusty London home, and quietly closed the door behind him. His secret would remain safe, known only to him. This beautiful world would remain untouched, a vibrant relic of a bygone era. Albert Phipps, the reclusive scholar, was content with his decision, for he had found a sanctuary, a realm of enchantment and wonder, where he was no longer a recluse. He was now an adventurer, an observer, and a guardian of an ancient world.

A WIZARDS TALE

CHAPTER 1

In a quiet hamlet, tucked away in the corners of an ancient kingdom, lived a young man named Finn. He was an unassuming character, known more for his keen intellect than his physical strength. Finn was a lover of lore, myths, and stories, especially those about the users of magic, the wizards.

One day, an elderly traveler arrived in the village. He was draped in long, flowing robes, adorned with symbols of power and arcane significance. His hair and beard were long and white, signaling his advanced age and accumulated wisdom. His deep-set eyes were twinkling as well as piercing, and they hinted at his vast knowledge and the mysteries he had learned and seen throughout his long life. He carried a tall staff with a glowing glass-like ball at its top, which was known to serve as a symbol of his power and a tool to channel his magic.

He said his name was Eamon, and he was searching for someone who could inherit his vast knowledge of magic and keep the flame alive. His voice had a harmonious rhythm, and his hands moved in graceful arcs, as if tracing unseen patterns in the air.

Watching and listening to Eamon caused Finn to be filled with many emotions. He felt fear of the wizard's power; he was excited about the possibility of becoming a great wizard, and he felt a degree of caution over the responsibility he was about to gain. Finally, he was curious and confused as to why he was chosen.

Eamon sensed all his concerns as he looked at Finn. "Finn I sense you are afraid. You have nothing to fear; I will not harm you or anyone around you."

I also sense that you do not know why you were chosen over all others in this world. I have known that my time here is ending and that I must find someone to carry on the responsibilities of the old order. For that reason, I have been walking the land for many years, seeking the right person. Up until now, I have failed.

"I am nothing special except I can read, write, and do simple numbers. I cannot do magic, and as far as I know, there is no one in my family who can do magic. The only magic I have seen, if you want to call it magic, is my father's ability to farm. He is very good at it," Finn said.

"Oh, my friend, you have more abilities than you can imagine. You are kind, patient, a quick learner, and you have a caring spirit. You know how to focus, and you intuitively know right from wrong. You show a strong spirit of curiosity combined with a creative manner of thinking. All of these attributes are important for becoming a master of magic. Having said that, do you wish to join me on this journey?" Eamon asked.

"I want to, but I need to help my father on the farm," Finn said.

"Let me talk with your parents," Eamon said.

Finn ran to the house and briefly told his parents what had happened. They followed him back to the field where Eamon stood.

"Welcome," Eamon said. "You have a very special son. I wish to share with him my skills so that he can follow in my footsteps, and I seek your approval."

Finn's parents looked at each other and looked back at the great wizard. "We are not a wealthy family. Finn is all the help we have. Without him, the farm may very well fail, and we would not live through the winter," Finn's father said.

"As long as your son is with me, your root cellar and larder will be full. Plant your fields, and they shall be productive." Eamon said. He raised his staff and said a few unintelligible words. The ball on top of his staff glowed a bright white, and then he slammed his staff into the ground. Finn and his family felt a slight quiver, then nothing.

"Look to your fields, then go to your cellar and see that I have spoken the truth," Eamon said.

Finn's mother and father looked at the fields and garden with awe. Here it was early spring, and the garden and fields were months ahead of where they should be. Finn's mother ran to the house. A few minutes later, she stood at the door and shouted, "The cellar and larder are, as he said, full to overflowing, and the cellar is as cool as it is in the winter time."

"I have kept my word; now if it is your son's wish, may we start our journey?" Eamon asked.

Finn's father looked at Finn. "Do you want to do this, son?"

"Yes, father," Finn said.

Putting his hand on his son's shoulder, he said, "Travel safely, and in everything you do, respect everything we are."

CHAPTER 2

Eamon and Finn spent days talking as they walked. From dawn to dusk, they discussed the lore of the land, the wisdom of the ancients, and the mysteries of magic. Eamon saw the spark in Finn he had been looking for.

For the next five years, they traveled the land from north to south and east to west. Finn learned how to control the four elements: wind, water, fire, and earth. He learned the runes and the words. He learned how to read truth and lies in people, and he learned how to talk to people's minds. He had not mastered these art forms as it would take many more years; however, even Eamon admitted that Finn had a great understanding of the magical arts.

On the anniversary of his sixth year with Eamon, he looked at Finn. "It is time for you to have a staff. It must be at least seven feet tall and be of oak." He turned around and started walking toward the forest. An hour later, they were deep in the forest, surrounded by many trees, none of which were oak.

Finn looked at Eamon. "We should look in another forest. These trees are pine and birch. This is a waste of time."

Eamon looked at Finn with a bit of distaste on his face. "Have I not told you about patience and focus? Focus, young man, and listen for the oak tree. It will call you when we are near."

They continued to walk for another two hours when Finn heard the most beautiful notes off to the west. He looked at Eamon and pointed to the sounds. With each step he took, the notes grew louder until, half an hour later, they stood before the most majestic oak tree he had ever seen.

In a quiet voice, Eamon said, "Talk to the tree. Tell it why you are here and that you are seeking a staff to hold a magic crystal. Ask it if it would be willing to sacrifice a straight, seven-foot branch for you to use. Speak to it respectfully. This is a very old and respected member of this forest."

Finn walked up to the tree, went down on one knee, placed his right hand on the tree's bark, and spoke softly. "Majestic and powerful Oak, I come before you as a simple apprentice of the wizard Eamon. He says that it is time for me to obtain a staff and that a staff from one of your branches would add great prestige to this lowly apprentice. Great Oak, would you please honor me with a seven-foot branch? It will be used to house a crystal befitting your sacrifice. I await your decision."

Several minutes went by, but nothing. Finn remembered Eamon's many admonitions about patience. Suddenly, the ground shook, and there was a crashing sound nearby.

About fifteen feet from where Finn stood was a seven-foot straight branch with enough knots in it to give it character.

Finn went over and picked up the branch. Eamon walked over to Finn. "We must now seek the crystal that will adorn your staff. That staff and crystal will amplify and focus your power. The place we seek is a four-day walk."

Saying that, Eamon turned and started walking. Finn followed close behind.

The four-day walk was unremarkable and really quite boring. The only thing that kept things somewhat mentally challenging was the practice of new and old magic.

About noon on the fourth day, they arrived at a creek that emptied into a river. Eamon turned away from the river. "The area we are looking for is about a kilometer up this creek."

The further they walked, the more they heard the rock chant. The closer they got, the louder the chant, and Finn noticed the rocks were a light blue and transparent. Eamon waded out into the creek, bent down, and started moving the rocks around. Within a few minutes he grunted and stood up. In his hand was a beautiful crystal-like stone. He walked over to Finn and handed him the crystal. Finn looked at it closely. It was a beautiful shade of blue and totally transparent. Eamon said, "Give me the staff and crystal to me." Placing the crystal on top of the staff, he said in a quiet voice, "Hanc crystal." With these words, tendrils came out of the staff and tightly secured the crystal to it. He handed the staff to Finn. Eamon continued to hold onto the staff as he said, "Haec baculus et crystallus Finnorum pertinent.

Mandatum ab aliquo non accipietis. Mandata Finnorum recipies, ea tantum exsequere et ut dicit versari." The crystal glowed brightly, and Finn felt a tremor in his hand, then his body briefly glowed with the same color as the crystal on his staff.

Eamon then moved his hand to Finn's shoulder and said, "Finn, receive the power and obligations of the old order. Will you use these powers for the greater good, to protect the weak, and to never use magic for personal gain?" Eamon asked.

"I will," Finn said. As he spoke the words, Finn felt a surge of power and confidence move through him, marking the beginning of his journey as a wizard of the old order.

At that point in time, they had spent more than six years together, and they both knew that Eamon's time was drawing to a close. Eamon's final lesson was about the greatest magic of all: life and death. He reminded Finn that every beginning has an end and that even magic couldn't interrupt the flow of natural life.

Suddenly, a glow encompassed Eamon, and his likeness slowly disappeared. As Finn watched Eamon disappear before him, a great sadness overtook him.

Finn had truly become a wizard. His journey had been filled with joy, wisdom, and sorrow, each moment shaping him into a magical guardian. He had learned the intricacies of magic, the wisdom of the ancients, and the meaning of responsibility. But above all, he understood that his journey was just beginning. As he held his staff high against the setting sun, he knew he was ready to fulfill his destiny.

MY WEIRD ROOMMATE

CHAPTER 1

It was my freshman year in college. I wasn't going to one of the big Ivy League colleges; it was a small private college located in Angwin, California. I received a Pell Grant and was accepted into their nursing program. My mother was a nurse and she impressed on me the academic rigors of becoming a registered nurse so I decided to rent a place off campus away from the chaos of dorms. California is not known for its cheap rents, so I knew it would be a tough search. Even with the grant money, I would have to get at least a part-time job to make ends meet.

A week before classes started, I drove up to Angwin to find a job and a place to live. I found a job at the PUC College Market as a bag boy. Finding a place to live, however, was a lot more difficult. Through the grapevine, I heard of a place across from the Chevron station on Brookside Park. When I met the landlord, surprisingly, I found out that the rent was well within my budget. One doesn't look a gift horse in the mouth, so I took it.

When I moved into my new rental, the landlord gave me a quirky smile and said, "The place comes with its quirks, but you'll get used to them!" I thought he was referring to the creaky floorboards or maybe the finicky bathroom faucet. As I expected, the wood floors creaked, and the windows were wavy, hinting at the home's age, but frankly, I was thrilled to have found such a treasure.

It turns out he wasn't talking about the floors or the bathroom faucet; it was about Gary.

Gary, as I found out, was the resident ghost, but I am getting ahead of myself.

A week after I moved in, I began to notice peculiar things. Items would shift from their original positions, the room's temperature would sporadically drop for no reason, and some nights I would hear a soft humming of an old tune I couldn't recognize.

One evening, after coming home late from work, I was startled to find a translucent figure standing in my living room. Based on the way he was dressed, the figure looked to be a young man from the 1960s. Needless to say, I yelped and the figure gave a slight, amused chuckle.

"Hello," the ghostly figure greeted, "sorry for the scare. My name's Gary."

It took me a minute or two before I regained my composure, and I replied, "Hi, Gary. You live here?"

"In a manner of speaking, yes," Gary replied. "I've been here for a long time."

I couldn't believe what I was seeing. I felt like Scrooge when he was confronted the ghost of Christmas present. I must be hallucinating. I'm tired, and the sandwich I had on the way home did taste a bit funny.

Rather than fool with this nonexistent ghost, I turned and headed for the bedroom. Once there, I turned on the light and shut the door. I didn't even get undressed; I just dropped on to my bed, pulled the pillow over my head, turned off the light, and tried to go to sleep. After what seemed like hours, sleep came.

The next morning was Saturday, so there were no classes. I got up, showered, put on fresh clothes, and slowly headed to the kitchen. On the kitchen table, I found my socks paired and neatly rolled up. The laundry that I had put in the dryer the day before was also sitting neatly folded on the kitchen table.

Odd, I was really tired last night; maybe I had been sleepwalking? I didn't want to tempt fate, so I picked up the clean laundry, took it back into the bedroom, and put it in the chest of drawers.

I walked back into the kitchen only to find that my blender had started making smoothies by itself. I knew I wasn't that forgetful. I hadn't put anything in the blender last night or this morning. I certainly had not turned it on.

A few minutes later, I saw pancake batter floating in the air, shaping itself into pancakes, and flipping over a non-existent flame. I blinked, rubbed my eyes, and tentatively said, "Hello?" Not knowing what to say, these words came out of my mouth. "Have a good sleep." A translucent hand gave me a thumbs up, and a voice chirped, "I hope you like blueberry!"

"Who or maybe what in the hell are you?" I asked.

"Didn't the landlord tell you? Wait, I bet he told you, 'The place comes with its quirks, but you'll get used to them!' speech.

Along with the squeaky floors and the dripping faucet, I am one of the quirks he was talking about. Let me reintroduce myself. I'm Gary, your roommate.

Sixty or so years ago, I was a student here. Unfortunately, I died in that bedroom. Not having any family, I was buried in a pauper's grave, and the next thing I knew, I was back in this house. For the most part, it has been lonely here. People just aren't used to ghosts as roommates. Girls are really the worst. A ghost who is a guy really puts them off. You seem pretty level-headed so I hope you stay longer than the last one. He barely made it through forty-eight hours," Gary said.

He may have been weird, but the guy, or ghost, could cook and clean.

Over time, I discovered Gary was quite the character. He had a thing for 80's music and would occasionally blast "Thriller" in the middle of the night (ironic, I know). He was also quite the prankster. He'd tie my shoelaces together, move my keys to the refrigerator, or set my alarm clock to quack like a duck. The truth is. I never really knew what was coming next.

One evening, after coming home from a particularly challenging day both at school and work, I found my living room transformed into a makeshift spa. There was calming music, floating candles (literally), and a note: "Thought you could use some R&R. P.S. The floating cucumber slices for your eyes are in the fridge. – Gary"

I couldn't help but chuckle.

The truth is, instead of being the creepy, lurking spirit you'd expect, Gary was more like an amusing roommate I never knew I needed. We'd have "movie nights" where I would turn on movies. Gary would toss popcorn into the air, letting it hover for a few seconds before dropping it into a bowl. Some nights, at first, we would sit and talk. He even helped me with course work. I did not realize that a ghost had a "photographic" memory. I would read a chapter to him, and he could quiz me with great ease.

I wasn't sure how friends and family would react to him, so I kept his presence a secret.

Believe it or not, he even helped in my effort to date. Being some what of a bookworm, my skills with women were limited. Gary, on the other hand, had been a player when he was alive. It's tough for you to understand, I know; however, I actually took dating advice from a ghost. Even with his help, I flopped on several occasions. There were times when he thought the girl was a loser or just not right for me. Then, without my permission, he would "intervene" and scare her off.

It soon got around that I wasn't the guy to date. Something was odd going on at my place. For that reason, a part of my junior year was a dating desert. Then it happened. One of my classmates, Jill, came up to me and said, "Hi. I was going to get a cup of coffee, and I wondered if you would like to join me. I know this is a bit forward, but that is just me. Don't feel pressured; you can say no, and I will understand. Oh, by the way, my name is Jill," she said.

Gary and I talked it over, and we decided we would introduce her to my "roommate."

I know you have other things to do, so let me make a long story short. Jill and I hit it off. When I invited her to the house, Gary pulled a couple of his "you don't belong here" stunts, and Jill wasn't really phased.

The introduction to Gary didn't create fear in her; rather, it created a sense of wonderment. Jill found, like I had, that living with a ghost wasn't so spooky. It was hilarious, unpredictable, and oddly comforting. As for those quirks the landlord mentioned, well, let's just say I wouldn't trade them for the world.

ABOUT THE AUTHORS

Webster (Russ) Russell and Dee Coffeen are well known authors of both fiction and non fiction books.

To date they have written six books, however they are best known for their young adult fantasy "Harry and the Stock Tank Dragon".

Even as "seniors", they lead an active life of writing, cruising, photography, and being with friends and family. They have been around the world three times, stepped on all seven continents, and visited over 100 countries.

If writing books and cruising were not enough to keep these two busy, they also author a cruising blog website, a NextDoor cruising page and create photo journals and videos of their world travels.

If you were to meet the many people throughout the world that know these two, they will tell you that they are fun, creative and curious, all great attributes of successful authors.

Russ and Dee make their home in central Texas and can be reached at russanddeebook@icloud.com.

Websites

Travel Blog & Photo Journals

https://russanddee.weebly.com

Books

https://authors-russanddee.weebly.com

Next Door Cruising Page

https://nextdoor.com/g/wakg7mrmk/